THE DRUMMOND BRAND

In Montana, settlers around the township of Bridger Butte were forced out by a ruinous winter. Their properties were bought by Luther Drummond, owner of the Diamond-D ranch, amid rumours that the settlers' misfortunes were attributable to Luther's son, Dagg. Embroiled in the town's affairs, Pinkerton detective Ethan Brodie is accused of murder and stagecoach robbery. Ethan and Claire Dumbril, the victim's daughter, vow to find the killers, but how will they fare and what perils await them?

WILLIAM DuREY

THE DRUMMOND BRAND

Complete and Unabridged

LINFORD
Leicester

First published in Great Britain in 2011 by
Robert Hale Limited
London

First Linford Edition
published 2012
by arrangement with
Robert Hale Limited
London

British Library CIP Data

DuRey, Will.
    The Drummond brand. - -
(Linford western library)
1. Western stories.
2. Large type books.
I. Title II. Series
823.9'2–dc23

ISBN 978–1–4448–1238–1

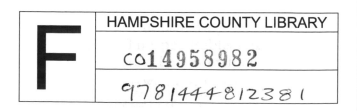
This book is printed on acid-free paper

For my sons,
Matthew and Philip

1

With the sleeves of her dress pushed back above her elbows, the woman brushed her brow with her bare forearm. The day was hot, but at this time of year heat came with the morning sun and clung on stubbornly long after the great orange orb had dropped behind the distant Rockies. The land cooled in the blackest part of the night but it never grew cold. Not even the infrequent rain shower caused a drop in temperature; it merely brought a momentary refreshment that disguised the pervasive heat. But there was no rain this day and the faultless blue sky offered no hint at such a possibility. Not that the woman was seeking any respite from the heat. She knew that the heat of a Montana summer was as extreme as the cold of a Montana winter. The hostility of the land and weather had been here before her and would still be here when she'd gone. Surviving was struggle enough without wasting energy wishing for what couldn't be altered.

She'd lived on this stretch of land most of her life. Lived in this very ranch house that had been built by her father and extended over the years by him and latterly her husband. It was a single storey building, which had spread outwards rather than upwards, the original building having been a simple cabin, the front part of which had been the living and cooking quarters while the rear part had been the sleeping area. That had been back in 1854 when the family had first settled in the valley. Now, almost thirty years later, the whole of the original cabin was a comfortable, well furnished living room on to which had been added three bedrooms and a cooking area. In addition, a bunkhouse had been erected some fifty yards away and stables and barns had been built as the ranch stock had developed.

The front of the ranch house faced west and an elevated porch had been constructed either side of the door. This provided a sitting place for those warm evenings when chores were completed and the long shadows to darkness stretched across the land. On the north side of the house a lean-to shelter had been added, a shaded place in which the woman could do the laundry away from the glare of the sun. It was in that shaded area that she now stood, wiping her brow and raising her gaze to the shimmering view of the distant, snow-topped mountains. It was a vista she loved and had done since the day her father had halted the team pulling their Connestoga wagon and declared they need travel no further. Time stood still whenever she paused to take in this view, momentarily, the everyday sounds of birdsong and lowing cattle were blotted from her consciousness. The heat was forgotten and she stood in a still and silent world. Then, the moment of relaxation over, one more arch of her back to ease those muscles which had tightened while bent over the wooden wash tub, she turned to gather up the pile of damp clothes. In this heat they would be dry almost before she hung them in a line.

She wasn't quite sure why she stopped and looked again beyond the rail that surrounded the ranch yard. Something had caught her attention out on the low ridge that was the main trail to the growing settlement of Bridger Butte. A movement. There it was again, something white momentarily showing against the green hillside. White, like snow sliding off a shovel, or a bough of blossom swaying in a breeze. There again. A shimmer. A horse's tail flicking away flies. And yes, a man, a motionless rider looking down on the ranch. She stayed in the shadow of the lean-to not knowing if from that distance — it was almost half a mile from the ridge to the ranch — he had seen her, but when he moved she knew he was heading in her direction.

The woman watched as the horse picked its way down the hillside to the flat pasture land that separated the ranch from the nearby hills. She recognized neither horse nor rider and, alone at the ranch house as she now was, experience demanded caution. Visitors to the ranch were rare and her pa had always cradled a rifle in his arms when a stranger rode in. The woman had no gun to hand so remained in the darkness at the side of the house and continued to watch as man and horse came closer. They approached slowly, walking, as though proving to the people at the ranch that they weren't a threat. The horse which, head-on, seemed to have no trace of white about it, carried its head high. Its neck and shoulders were thick and gave the impression of a beast with stamina. Its gait was steady, its stride long. The man on its back barely moved. Little could be seen of his face because the high domed hat he wore cast a shadow down to his lips. He wore a tough cotton shirt which was blue and fastened at the neck with a criss-crossed black lace. When he got to the gateway he tugged gently on the reins and brought the horse to a standstill. He leaned forward, rested his left hand on his saddle pommel and slapped at the horse's neck with his right. It wasn't a heavy slap, but dust rose from the beast's body like flour from worn sack.

'Didn't expect to see a ranch out here,' he called, making it clear that he knew the woman was standing in the shadows. He looked back to the ridge. 'If that trail yonder doesn't lead to Bridger Butte then I'm lost.'

Like his approach to the ranch, the rider's speech was unthreatening. It was neither spoken too fast nor a drawl. His tone and words carried enough humour to dispel most of the caution that experience had schooled into the woman. 'You're not lost,' she said, stepping into the yard so she could be seen. 'Bridger Butte is another six or so miles.'

The man removed his hat and wiped the dampness from his forehead with his sleeve. He was younger than the woman had supposed him to be, younger than her by five or six years. His face was weather beaten and it and his clothes were as dusty as his horse. The horse, now that she saw it from the side, was a confusion of colour. It had a sorrel head and front body with white hindquarters, mane and tail. Here and there, splotches of the front colour appeared further along its back, like a painter had used its rump to clean his brush. She'd never before seen a horse with such unique markings and up close she confirmed her first impression that it was a strong horse bred for endurance. The man had attended to it continuously while he'd spoken to the woman, not only patting its neck and shoulder but also reaching forward and gently tugging its ear to show he was pleased with it. She liked that, a sign that his horse was important to him.

'There's water in the trough over there if your horse needs a drink,' she said, 'and you're welcome to help yourself from that gourd in the shade. I just pulled it from the well a few minutes ago. It'll still be cold.'

The man nodded, an appreciation of the offer. He stepped down from the saddle, opened the gate and led the horse through. 'Kind of you, ma'am,' he said. 'My name's Ethan Brodie.'

'I'm Ellen Hartley.'

'I thought all the ranches were on the other side of the Dearborn.'

'All except this one,' she told him, then, with a tight little smile that tried to hold back her pride, she added, 'and this one was here first.'

The water trough was sited under a hitching rail and Ethan looped the reins twice around the long pole and stood for a moment while the horse lapped at the water.

'He's thirsty,' said Ellen Hartley.

'We've covered a lot of ground since

sunup,' he explained, 'but he wouldn't be so hot if we'd hit the Dearborn an hour ago as I expected.'

'You're new to the territory?'

'First time this far north.'

'Looking for work?'

'No, ma'am. Just visiting. Someone to see.'

'Extra hands will soon be needed on the ranches hereabout. Nearly time to bring the steers down from the hills. My husband'll be wanting someone if you're interested.' Ethan shook his head but Ellen carried on talking, not really hoping to persuade him to accept employment, just reluctant to let him go without further conversation. She was surprised by how easily she had taken to Ethan Brodie. It wasn't that he'd done or said anything special, but his demeanour inspired confidence. He was unhurried in everything he did as though sure that whatever he hoped to achieve would be done with quiet efficiency. 'My husband will be back soon. Can you stay and take a meal

9

with us? I know John will enjoy having someone new to talk to. Since the fight at the Little Bighorn even visits from army patrols seem to have dried up.'

'Very kind of you, Mrs Hartley, but me and the horse have been travelling a few days now. We'd like to get the journey finished as soon as possible. I'll just take that drink of cold water and we'll be on our way.'

Her shy smile was an acknowledgement of defeat and she walked with him to the lean-to where he drank deeply from the earthenware jug. He splashed a little on a hand and rubbed it over his face, clearing away some surface dust but making what was left behind on the edges of his face all the more obvious. 'Did you say six miles to Bridger Butte?'

'Once you've cleared that hump-backed ridge,' she pointed in the direction he would be taking, 'you'll come to the river. There isn't a bridge but it's not running high. Just follow the trail for the best crossing point.

After that, at a canter, it'll take forty minutes.' They walked back to the water trough and he swung up into the saddle. In as undemonstrative a manner as he could muster, Ethan Brodie tugged at the brim of his hat. It was a gesture not just of farewell but also of gratitude for the hospitality and plea- sure for the company. Such minimal action, of course, was not Ellen Hartley's way, but she almost surprised herself when she spoke. 'If you're staying around a while do come and visit, Mr Brodie. And remember there's a job here if you want it.' She flushed slightly at her forwardness. Hiring and firing had always been her husband's task. Ethan Brodie clicked his tongue, a message to his mount, which was reinforced by the pressure of his heels. The horse walked forward towards the gate.

'Mr Brodie,' Ellen Hartley called and ran to catch up to him before the gate was closed again. 'After you cross the river don't stray from the trail. You'll be on Diamond-D land. They aren't tolerant of trespassers even if it's accidental.'

Ethan's brow was etched with a crease. 'Diamond-D? I thought Drummond's land was the other side of Bridger Butte.'

Ellen was curious as to how Ethan Brodie knew who owned the Diamond-D brand and the location of his main spread, but it didn't prevent her giving the information he sought. 'He's just acquired the land across the river. Bought out Siggi Larrsen last week.'

Ethan Brodie tugged again at his hat brim. 'Obliged for the information, Mrs Hartley.' This time when he clucked at the horse and pressed with his heels Ellen Hartley sensed a degree of urgency in his action. In addition, she thought his expression had lost a little of its warmth. She stood at the gate for several minutes, marking the progress of Ethan Brodie to the trail along the ridge by the startling white hindquarters of his mount.

2

Not since leaving his parent's Missouri farm on the Ozark plateau had Ethan Brodie called any place home. For some years he'd wandered the mid-west states working on cattle ranches, labouring in sawmills, hauling goods from depots to growing settlements and, for a short period, had cut hair and supplied bath water in a canvas town in Colorado where a silver strike petered out before anyone got rich. At that time, Ethan Brodie was happy to do anything that flipped a few honest dollars in his pocket and demanded nothing more of him than that he supply the day of labour for which he was being paid. He'd seen the vast ranges of the Texas Panhandle and the fertile Californian valleys, areas that were El Dorado for cattle barons and crop growers but hadn't proved preferable to Ethan to the movement of a good horse under him. He'd seen them and moved on, happy to live each day as it came and roam the big country, accepting whatever life threw at him at the next town or over the next hill.

Even when he finally accepted a permanent job it didn't mark the end of his travels, nor did he consider the rooms he'd rented for the past four years as home. They were nothing more than a functional base close to the offices of his employer, a location of acceptable comfort between assignments. As an agent of the Pinkerton Detective Agency he was deployed on cases throughout the states served by the Kansas Pacific railroad.

But Ethan had never ridden north of the Oregon Trail. In his years as a saddle tramp, the land of the Yellowstone and Powder Rivers had been home to restless Indian tribes and, at that time, though he didn't consider himself a coward, he couldn't view the prospect of skirmishes with hostile bands as anything but foolish. The discovery of gold in the Black Hills had tempted many men north but, to Ethan's knowledge, panning rivers had made few men rich. The lure of gold wasn't worth risking the wrath of the tribesmen and, as a young man, he knew of no other inducement that could. Since then, since Custer's defeat at the Little Bighorn, most warriors had settled on government reservations. Now all territory of the United States of America was available for settlement and development.

As he sat on the humpback mound above the Dearborn with the snow topped mountains of the Bitterroot Range to his left and the river running away to the flat prairie land to his right, Ethan Brodie was surprised by the thoughts in his head. A group of five pronghorn were drinking downstream. One looked his way in nervous curiosity but dipped its head to the water again before walking gingerly to the cover of trees. For three days, since leaving Billings, he'd journeyed through similar country. It was unlike any he'd seen in his ten years of travel. The gentle sweeps of the low hills were covered with cottonwood trees and tall cedars. Wherever he'd ridden he'd seen an abundance of game, herds of pronghorn deer darting among the trees or sometimes merely grazing by a river. There had been elk and bear — even the scent of the latter was enough to spook his stallion. The grass land was lush and the rivers he'd crossed were clear and cool and full of fish that were big enough to provide a satisfying meal. This was land on which a man could settle, land where he could raise stock or grow crops. Land on which he could build a home.

Ellen Hartley had told the truth about the Dearborn River: it wasn't running high. When Ethan Brodie rode across, the deepest part was no more than hock high. The far side was a long, steady climb through a forested slope but the trail was well defined. Ethan had just reached the tree line when he heard the gunshot. The report seemed to still the hillside. Bird song ceased; even the breeze held still, killing the sough as it troubled the branches of the surrounding tall cedars. He reined in, reached forward to rest a hand on the animal's neck and waited to see if more gunshots would follow.

After a couple of minutes, with no repetition of the harsh disturbance and the sounds of the forest returning to the commonplace, Ethan urged his horse forward. They travelled cautiously, at walking pace, Ethan listening and watching for whoever had discharged the gun. A hunter, he supposed, garnering fresh meat for the pot, but in a strange country it didn't pay to take anything for granted. Also, Ellen Hartley's warning about the territory across the river echoed in his mind.

His supposition that the shot had been fired by a hunter proved unfounded when he came across a group of men as he rounded a bend in the trail. Three of the men were mounted, the fourth stood over the sprawled body of his dead mount. The horse had a broken leg and a bullet in its brain. The man afoot had a rifle in his hand and an angry look on his face. He was a thickset man of fair complexion and clean shaven. He was a year or two over thirty and wore typical cowboy garb; leather chaps over dark, cord trousers and a single holster gunbelt around his waist. His shirt was plain, off-white calico and a navy 'kerchief hung in heavy folds on his chest. His hat, which had parted company with his head, was light grey and dangled down his back by means of a thick black cord.

It was clear to Ethan that whatever business the group was about, it was now in limbo because of the dead horse. Whether they were waiting for the unhorsed man's temper to abate or whether they deferred to him for another reason, it was obvious the mounted men weren't moving on until he was ready. The man worked the mechanism of his rifle ensuring there was another bullet in the breech. For a moment it looked as though he was going to shoot the dead animal again. A rider spoke. His voice was soft and low and held a hint of mockery. 'It's dead.'

The words didn't appease the man afoot. His face grew redder, his mouth twisted in a snarl. 'I know it's dead.' He kicked the carcass.

'Then let's get going,' said the rider.

The man glared, convinced that he was being mocked but too angry to form a response. At that moment, however, a rider at the back of the group saw Ethan Brodie. He pushed his horse forward so that he came abreast of the man who'd been doing the talking. 'Hey,' he said, and nodded in Ethan's direction.

All eyes looked down the trail to study Ethan who was still approaching at a walk.

'Hey, you.' The man afoot advanced

down the trail. The riders followed him, spreading out in a line and looping round Ethan in a half circle. 'I need that horse.'

'So do I,' replied Ethan, 'and he's mine.' Ethan kept his voice low and firm trying not to show the unease he felt. He didn't like the way he was being surrounded nor the rifle in the man's hands. He transferred the reins to his left hand and let his right hand rest on the butt of his Colt.

'Get off him, cowboy,' said the man, bringing the barrel of the rifle round in a slow arc to point at Ethan's midriff.

'Horse stealing's a hanging offence in every other territory I've been through. Don't suppose it's any different here.' Ethan spoke with more confidence than he felt.

'Ain't stealing your horse,' said the man, 'I'm confiscating it.' Some of the other men grinned.

'Care to explain that to me?' Ethan asked.

'Simple,' said the man. 'You're

trespassing. This is Diamond-D land.'

'This is a public trail,' argued Ethan. 'No one has the right to call it their land.'

'Looks like we've got a lawyer here,' said the man, looking around at the other horsemen who laughed and grinned accordingly.

'No lawyer,' said Ethan, 'but I ain't causing any trouble. You've got no right to accuse me of anything.'

'Sure I have,' the man snapped. 'You've scared the cattle we were rounding up. Scattered them back to the hills. Perhaps you're planning to round them up yourself and run them across the river. Rustling's a hanging offence, too. But if we confiscate your horse you won't be able to rustle any cattle. Think of it as being saved from a hangman's rope.' Again the mounted men laughed.

'You're not getting my horse,' said Ethan. 'You've got no more right to take it than Luther Drummond has the right to close the road.'

'That so,' said the man. 'Charlie,' he called, 'show the cowboy what constitutes our right to his horse.'

Before the man had finished speaking a lasso was thrown over Ethan's head by a rider who had circled round behind. It was pulled taut, pinning Ethan's arms to his side and tightening as he struggled. With a sharp pull he was dragged over the back of his horse and hit the dry ground hard. With the breath knocked out of him, his shoulder ached where he'd landed and the friction of the rope burned his arms. With difficulty, he made several attempts to get to his feet. Each time, Charlie yanked on the rope and toppled him face down to the ground.

Eventually, Ethan got himself to a sitting position but no matter how hard he struggled he couldn't free his arm. The man with the rifle approached and crashed the butt end into Ethan's chest, knocking him on to his back. 'Now you understand,' the man said standing astride Ethan, 'this is Diamond-D land.

Drummond's kingdom. His range and his law.' He reached down, removed the Colt from Ethan's holster and threw it into the nearby bushes. Then he stepped back. 'All right, Charlie. Let him go.'

Charlie relaxed his grip on the rope so that Ethan could ease his arms free and lift the loop over his head. Every movement produced a spasm of pain and he wondered what damage had been caused by the blow to his chest with the rifle. He struggled to his feet, his anger exacerbated by pain and humiliation.

'Now,' the man said, 'this horse is mine. It's on Diamond-D land so it's Diamond-D property.' He turned and grabbed the saddle horn ready to mount. Though he knew he didn't stand any chance of success against four men, Ethan wasn't prepared to lose his horse without a fight. He ran at the man who, hearing a shouted warning from one of the riders, turned back to fend off the attack. Ethan threw a right hand punch but, forewarned, the man was able to turn his head away from it and take it on the shoulder. In return, he jabbed a short right punch of his own which, in other circumstances wouldn't have carried enough weight to trouble Ethan, however it caught him in the chest, almost exactly on the same point that the rifle butt had landed, and an explosion of pain shot through his body. He staggered back. The man came after him and threw a punch at his jaw, which put Ethan on the ground again. He was having difficulty breathing, only able to take in small gasps of air because every movement of his chest elicited another wave of pain. Ethan struggled once more to his feet, reluctant to admit defeat, reluctant to lose his horse, glaring hostility at the man opposite but unable to see any means of continuing the fight.

Charlie resolved the dilemma. Riding his horse up close he used its flank to propel Ethan towards his opponent. Surprised and overpowered by the weight of the horse, Ethan stumbled on to the man's short punch into his solar plexus. On the way down a vicious punch landed on the side of his jaw and for some moments he lost consciousness.

When he came to it was to discover he had been tied between two trees. A rope attached to each wrist was secured to the lowest branches but they were still high enough to pull his arms above head height and his body extended so that his feet barely touched the ground. The man approached astride Ethan's horse. 'This is your last warning, cowboy,' he said. 'If I catch you on Diamond-D land again, I'll kill you.'

Ethan's agony was both physical and mental but as he listened to the riders heading back down the trail to the river he vowed to himself he would have his revenge.

3

After leaving Bridger Butte, the stagecoach to Billings took a western loop to collect passengers from the smaller settlement of Enterprise before hitting the southbound road. It met the lower trail, the one Ethan Brodie had used as his route to Bridger Butte, a mile or so north of a natural cutaway through the foothills of the Bitterroot Mountains. This place was known as Gunner Pass and Gunner Pass was the destination of the four riders.

Once across the river, they backtracked Ethan Brodie's progress, riding the ridge past the Hartley spread without sparing the ranch buildings as much as a glance. The incident on the far bank of the Dearborn had cost a lot of time and if they were to get to Gunner Pass before the stage they hadn't a moment more to lose. Dagg

Drummond, Luther's son, the man astride Ethan's stallion, was having a difficult ride. He'd lived on a ranch all his life, had worked with beeves and horses since he was a boy, but had no affinity with any animal. In truth, he was nervous of high spirited horses. When his father had grown too old for breaking in new stock the task had fallen to the foreman and other hired help. Dagg was happy enough to ride docile beasts which were schooled in the ways of a good working cow pony. There was a corral full of them at the Diamond-D, unspectacular saddle horses that turned quickly when rounding up cattle, worked quietly all day on the range, but seldom moved faster than a granny in a rocking chair.

This beast was different. When Dagg touched his spurs to its flanks it burst forward with an unnerving surge of speed. Dagg's reaction was to haul back on the reins, consequently pulling the horse's head high, almost making it rear, almost bringing it to a standstill.

Dagg cursed, and holding the reins short and tight by the animal's neck, he slapped its flank hard with the excess leather. These were mixed signals to the horse — the slaps urging it forward, the short rein holding it to the spot. Confused, it snorted and stamped and turned a full circle, allowing the other riders to pass and get some yards ahead. Dagg's temper, on a short fuse from the moment his original mount had broken a leg, welled within him. He didn't like anything or anyone to publicly highlight his failings. He was a Drummond and expected to be the master in all situations, expected instant obedience from man and beast.

Pricked once more with the spurs, the horse reacted as it had the first time, lunging forward, lengthening its stride running at full gallop almost instantly. Dagg Drummond hung on, battling with the dilemma of stopping to swap horses with one of his men, thereby advertising his discomfort with a strong horse, or persevere and risk the ignominy of being thrown from the saddle. He chose the latter and rode the miles to Gunner Pass trying to disguise his own inability by brutal treatment of the horse. Unaccustomed to such roughness, the stallion sped across the country, its white tail swishing like the surrender banner of a defeated army.

The last part of the journey from Enterprise to the junction was a long decline down which a driver of any coach or wagon had to work hard to keep his team in check. When Dagg Drummond and his men reached the junction they were several minutes ahead of the stage and could see it rocking and swaying, while behind, a cloud of grey dust rose higher than the vehicle. Above the approaching sound of iron clad hoofs, iron clad wheels and complaining coach, the voice of the driver calling to his charges carried to them down the channel of the valley. They pushed their own mounts forward and, when they reached the confines of Gunner Pass, in accordance with the prearranged plan, guided them among the bushes at either side of the trail.

Although Dagg hadn't taken the trouble to change saddles, he had remembered to transfer the bundle that had been tied behind the saddle on his dead horse. It was a blanket with a hole in the middle wide enough for his head to go through. Each man had one, draping it over his shoulders to hide his clothing. Then he checked his pistol. Satisfied that he carried a fully loaded weapon, he covered the lower part of his face with his 'kerchief and pulled his hat low on his brow so that the only feature to be seen by the folks on the stage would be eyes in deep shadow. As the stage slowed when it came into the Pass, they were ready.

Dagg rode into the road some thirty yards ahead of the coach and discharged his pistol into the air. 'Hold those horses, driver,' he yelled, then fired again.

The driver dragged back on the reins.

'Whoa,' he shouted and clamped his foot on the brake. The horses slithered and snorted and tangled with each other as they tried to halt with the urgency demanded by their driver. The front two bumped together and the one nearest Dagg almost lost its footing as the impetus from behind countered its own effort to stop.

The frenzied motion of the coach made it impossible for the guard to use his shotgun. There was as much likelihood of shooting one of the horses as hitting the outlaw in the middle of the road. By the time the jerking and bouncing of the vehicle had ceased the other three bandits had emerged from hiding and had him covered with their own weapons. The guard put his rifle down into the well below his feet. They weren't carrying enough money to die for.

'Throw down the strong box,' Dagg called.

The guard, a round-faced man with a ruddy complexion and stubby grey whiskers that were stained with chewing tobacco, pulled the metal box out from under his feet and threw it on the ground. 'Can we go now?' he asked.

'I'll tell you when,' growled Dagg.

Two of the other riders dismounted and took the box off to the side of the trail. One of them used his hand gun to break the lock. Inside was a couple of bundles of paper money and some documents. The man stuffed the money inside his shirt. 'Not much here,' he told Dagg.

'Of course not,' scolded the guard. 'Every durn fool knows that the big bucks are when we're going the other way. The only time the box is full is when we're bringing in a payroll for the logging camp.' He worked his mouth and spat on the ground as if to show his disgust at their incompetence.

'In that case,' said Dagg, 'we'll just have to see what your passengers are carrying.' He motioned to the other bandit who had dismounted. 'Get them out here.'

'Hey,' protested the guard. 'Those people are paying passengers. You've got the strong box. Leave them alone.'

'Shut up, old man,' said Dagg.

The guard opened his mouth as if he was going to continue the argument but no words came out. Instead, a quizzical expression crossed his face fleetingly as though something had occurred to him, as though he recognized the words, or the voice or the manner of speaking were familiar to him. Hadn't someone called him *old man* just last night? Someone who had found it just as difficult to hide his contempt. He gazed at Dagg as though trying to see his features despite the bandanna around his face, then his gaze moved to each of the other bandits as though seeking something that would confirm his suspicion. He found it when he finally alighted on the one who had come from the bushes at the side of the trail and who still remained astride his horse. In fact it was the horse that grabbed his attention and retained it long enough for his expression to change to one of certain knowledge. He checked the other horses in a manner all too obvious to escape the hold-up leader's notice. Dagg knew exactly what the old man had seen. Boldly, on the rump of the horses of the other three riders, was emblazoned the brand of the Diamond-D.

The guard pointed at Dagg. 'Hey, you're — '

Dagg Drummond responded the only way he could. 'Don't go for that gun, old man,' he yelled, but even as he was shouting the lie he was firing two shots into the guard's chest. Soundlessly, the guard fell backwards, dead before he landed across the driver's thighs.

'Why d'ya do that?' complained the shocked driver. 'He wasn't going for any gun. That was murder.'

'Shutup,' snapped Dagg, 'or you'll be next.' He signalled to the mounted rider to take the horse to the back of the coach, away from any other observant eyes. 'Get those passengers out the coach,' ordered Dagg.

'This is it,' said the man first instructed to empty the stage. 'There's only these three. Right gents, let's have everything you're carrying.'

Having witnessed the violence perpetrated against the guard, the three men seemed only too eager to hand over what little money they claimed to be carrying. The first man was a supervisor at the logging camp who had been summoned to the head office in Billings. His billfold was the heaviest, containing almost two hundred dollars. His intention had been to paint the town red while he was there.

The second man had only a handful of greenbacks pushed loosely in his jacket pocket. He was going, he told them, to his brother's funeral and had barely been able to raise the money to make the trip. His well worn clothes testified to the fact that he wasn't a rich man.

At first glance, the third man could

have been mistaken for some kind of drummer. He wore a new Derby hat and a brown, store-bought suit the lapels of which he clutched in his hands as though he was some politician preparing to give a speech. But on closer inspection, physically, he had the sun ripened face and broad chest of an outdoor man — a farmer, cow herder or timber jack — fresh from the barber's parlour. There was bath tub cleanliness about him and his jaw shone with applied aftershave lotion, its perfume as pungent to his fellow passengers as that of the sweating horses to their driver. Despite the authority that, initially, his garb bestowed on him, it was clear that the situation left him ill at ease. He fidgeted with his clothes, his hands straying from jacket lapels to the bottom of his waistcoat. He tugged sharply, stronger than was necessary to remove the wrinkles from sitting, almost as though he was trying to pull it down to his hips. His right hand moved wide across his stomach, like a man accustomed to protecting himself, expecting to feel the leather of a gunbelt and, somewhere within reach, the handle of a six-gun. But this proving fruitless he pressed his arm against his side. Anyone watching him closely might have assumed his surreptitious actions were to assure himself of the presence of a Colt in a shoulder holster. When it came to his turn to hand over his money, the nearest outlaw made exactly that assumption.

'If you're carrying a weapon under your coat you'd better chuck it now.' The passenger didn't respond, just dropped his gaze to the road, seemingly determined not to engage in conversation with the outlaws. His adversary's retort was sudden and brutal. Slashing the barrel of his pistol down on the man's shoulder, he caused the man to stagger backwards until he collided with the stagecoach. Swiftly and angrily, the bandit stepped forward, grabbed the passenger by the front of his coat and slammed him once more against the coach. Then he pulled aside the jacket, laying open to examination what was concealed beneath.

To the bandit's surprise there was nothing; no pistol tucked into the waistband of the man's trousers and no under arm holster. This didn't appease the outlaw. Instead of the lack of weapons rendering the passenger less of a threat it seemed to have a wholly different reaction on the robber, as though being unarmed was a source of mockery. Roughly, using the hand that held his gun, he backhanded the passenger across the mouth, ripping his lips and cheeks and launching a gout of blood through the air. The passenger's legs buckled and he almost sank to the ground. Using the stagecoach to support him, he remained on his feet and wiped the blood from his face with his left hand. Determination flared in his eyes, a message that he'd taken all he intended to take.

'Your money,' said the outlaw, waving his gun threateningly. 'Come on. Hand it over.'

The passenger pulled a slim wallet from an inside pocket and threw it on the ground.

Dagg Drummond eased his horse forward and looked at the leather billfold. 'How much is in there?'

'Fifty dollars,' said the passenger, his swelling mouth making it difficult to form coherent words.

Dagg Drummond laughed, a sound of pure contempt. 'Fifty dollars! Well. I'm sure a well-dressed business man like yourself is travelling with a lot more than fifty dollars.'

'That's all I'm carrying,' said the passenger and he turned out his pockets to prove they were empty.

'We don't have time to dawdle,' said Dagg. Indicating the assortment of the bags and cases on the coach roof, he threw a question at the driver. 'Does he have luggage up there?'

'That stuff's protected by — ' Dagg

Drummond didn't say anything, just pulled back the hammer of his Colt and pointed it at the driver's head. The driver quit talking, crawled on to the roof and threw down a substantial carpet bag. 'Sorry,' he said to the passenger who seemed now to be in a lot of discomfort from the blow he'd taken in the face.

'That all there is?' inquired Dagg.

'That's it,' said the driver.

The outlaw who'd dished out the violence knelt beside the bag and, finding that a key was required to remove a small lock, produced a knife from a scabbard on his belt and sliced through the fabric of the bag. He tipped the contents on the road and sorted through them. 'Nothing here,' he said after a brief search. 'No money.'

'Where is it?' snapped Dagg.

'There isn't any,' said the passenger.

'Don't lie,' said Dagg. 'You wouldn't be travelling without it.'

The man looked at the mounted outlaw leader, gazed at him as the guard had, as though trying to recognize the face below the wide-brimmed hat and the high covering neckerchief. Gazed at him as though hoping to prove the identity of the man he suspected him to be. 'I don't know what you're talking about,' he said. His arms hung at his sides, not loosely, but with a certain rigidity, like he was holding himself in readiness to launch an attack, or a defence.

The stance didn't escape Dagg's observation. He chuckled. 'It's under his shirt,' he announced. 'He's wearing a belt under his shirt.'

Even though Dagg had suspected the passenger was preparing to launch an attack, the suddenness, when it came, still caught him off guard. The man sprang forward, rushing the nearest outlaw, the one who had searched his bag. He was still on one knee and had re-holstered his pistol while going through the man's belongings. The man kicked him hard in the face as he tried to reach the cover of the bushes. The outlaw grunted in pain but was quick enough to catch the passenger's leg and throw him to the ground. For several seconds they grappled, rolling on the hard, dusty road, neither gaining mastery, both forgetting, in the urgency of the moment, what those watching were unable to — the fact that, ultimately, the passenger couldn't win.

A series of rolls took the antagonists, at one moment, under the wheels of the stagecoach, and the next, close to the hoofs of the bandits' horses. Somehow, the passenger emerged from this maul with a substantial rock in his hand. He hit the outlaw once, above the left eye, splitting the skin so that blood spurted immediately, then again, on the left cheek, which ended the outlaw's resistance. The passenger raised the rock for a third blow when Dagg Drummond fired two bullets into his chest, killing him instantly.

'Don't just stand there,' the outlaw leader yelled. 'Get the money and let's ride.'

While the outlaw who had been fighting scrambled unsteadily to his feet, the other one who had dismounted ripped the dead man's shirt apart and found a linen money belt beneath. He untied it, slung it over his shoulder then helped his companion on to his horse. In moments the four bandits were galloping south along the road to Billings.

4

At about the moment Dagg Drummond fired his gun to halt the Billings
bound stagecoach, Ellen Hartley was
cutting through the ropes that sus-
pended the bruised and bleeding Ethan
Brodie. 'Something's amiss,' she'd told
her husband fifteen minutes earlier
when he'd arrived at the ranch house.
She was still watching the wispy dust
trail heading south along the ridge
when he'd ridden in for his midday
meal. He'd listened to her story about
the visit of Ethan Brodie on his
distinctive horse and how, as she'd
finished off the laundry in the shade of
the lean-to, she'd seen that same horse
ridden once more along the ridge but in
the opposite direction to Bridger Butte.

Ellen's husband dismissed her concern. A small rancher had enough to
occupy his mind without getting

involved in the coming and going of a stranger. 'Man's just changed his mind. Expect he met someone on the trail who told him that Bridger Butte is a deadbeat settlement. Now he's heading back to Billings.'

'Mr Brodie said there was someone in Bridger Butte that he had to see. He didn't seem like the sort of man who would abandon a mission because of a chance meeting with someone on the trail. Besides . . . ' She let the word hang, reluctant to finish what she was going to say. Instead she reached for the cloth John would use to dry himself once he'd sluiced the morning's sweat and grime from his hands and face.

Taking the towel from her he prompted her to continue. 'Besides what?'

Because he'd asked her for more details, her reluctance evaporated. 'When he stopped here on his way to Bridger Butte he was alone, but there were four riders heading south.'

'So what are you worrying about?'

said John Hartley as he'd flipped the dirty water into the dust of the yard. 'He met up with those he came to see.'

'I don't think so,' said Ellen. 'Although I recognized the horse, I don't think that Mr Brodie was the rider.'

'Well who was riding it? Did you recognize the men?'

That was the problem for Ellen. Instinct had told her they were Diamond-D riders. Telling that to John would shatter any hope for assistance from him. She knew he wasn't prepared to risk confrontation with the Diamond-D, wasn't going to give Luther Drummond reason to focus on this spread as he'd done with some of the smaller ranches north of Bridger Butte. 'He went across the river,' was all she said, her voice low and deliberate. John Hartley turned his head in that direction, understanding the meaning of her words. 'I think something's wrong,' she added.

'No doubt we'll find out soon

enough,' replied her husband as he'd walked into the house.

Following, Ellen had filled a tin plate with stew from a black pot and poured thick coffee into a tin mug. She'd put the food and drink on the table for him but had set no place for herself. Instead, after he'd eaten a couple of forkfuls, she'd left the house and made her way to the stable. Quickly she'd harnessed their bay filly, backed her between the poles of their buggy and was soon racing away towards the Dearborn.

At the sound of horse and buggy in motion, John had rushed outside but Ellen was out of earshot by the time he'd gained the porch. He could only watch with a sense of foreboding as the buggy threw up its slipstream of grit and dust.

Ethan was conscious when Ellen came across him. Indeed, he'd heard the ruckus of the fast moving vehicle long before the buggy came into view. He'd shouted when he figured the driver was within hailing distance but it was quite unnecessary. The watchful Ellen Hartley had already spotted him and was pulling hard on the reins to halt the galloping bay.

Arms aching, chest sore and bumps on his head swelling and discolouring, Ethan sat on the ground. Dousing his neckerchief with water she'd brought in a canteen, Ellen used it to wash the blood from his face. Few words were exchanged, Ellen concentrating as she dabbed at his cuts and he silent because the anger inside him was filling his mouth with profanities such as he chose not to utter around any woman.

Eventually, when she was sure the bleeding had stopped, she rinsed the neckerchief free of blood stains with the last of the water and gave it back to Ethan. 'Come,' she said, 'I've got a salve at the house that'll help those cuts to heal.'

'Have you got a saddle horse back there I can borrow?'

Ethan asked. 'I'll pay for the loan of him.'

His eyes were dark, his mouth a firm, thin line of determination. It was clear to Ellen Hartley that his physical pain had, for the moment, been suppressed by his anger. 'We can talk about that back at the ranch,' she said.

'No, Mrs Hartley. My horse has been stolen. I want him back.'

'I know they took your horse,' she said. 'I saw it. That's why I'm here.'

The meaning behind her words surprised him. 'You came looking for me?'

'There were four of them,' she explained, 'and I didn't think you'd give up your horse without a fight.'

'How long ago did you see them?'

'Thirty minutes,' she replied. 'They were on the trail past the ranch house. Heading south.'

'Did you recognize them, Mrs Hartley?'

Slowly, Ellen shook her head, but her denial wasn't convincing. Ethan, however, was already indebted to her, and that, for the moment, forbade him from questioning her further. With an agility that disguised the spasms of pain and general discomfort, the residue of the beating he'd taken, Ethan sprang to his feet. He scavenged around the nearby bushes until he found his hat and discarded pistol. With each of those items restored to its rightful place and his damp neckerchief tied around his neck, he clambered on to the buggy alongside his rescuer and they returned swiftly to the Hartley ranch.

John Hartley watched from the porch as the buggy came through the gateway into the ranch yard. He stepped forward to grip the bay's bridle so that his wife could step to the ground without mishap. Introductions were made and Ethan's gratitude for Ellen's intervention expressed.

Inside the ranch house, Ellen busied herself with heating the coffee pot and discovering on a high shelf in the cooking room the jar of salve she sought. Meanwhile, Ethan was laying out twenty dollars for the hire of John Hartley's best saddle horse, rig and rifle. 'I'll bring them all back,' the newcomer told the rancher. 'They can't be an hour ahead and if your horse is fresh I should be able to close the distance between us quickly.'

Just then, Ellen returned to the room. Her face betrayed her anxiety. 'Be careful,' she told Ethan. 'They don't tolerate anyone who opposes them.' She flushed deeply, realizing instantly that, despite her earlier denial, she had betrayed the fact that she knew who had attacked him.

Ethan spoke calmly, as though he hadn't noticed her slip, hoping to smooth over her embarrassment. 'I know they were Diamond-D riders,' he explained. 'One of them kept telling me I was trespassing on Diamond-D land which gave him the authority to take my horse.'

John Hartley rose to his feet. He wasn't angry that his wife had taken it upon herself to intervene on Ethan

Brodie's behalf, after all, Ellen was a strong willed woman and helping out neighbours was something she'd done all her life. But this man wasn't a neighbour and his dispute was with the Drummonds. No one within a hundred miles of Bridger Butte chose to oppose the Drummonds. Perhaps, two days ago, John Hartley wouldn't have given any thought to a stranger being beaten up by Diamond-D riders, would have let his wife patch him up and send him on his way, but that was before yesterday's uneasy confrontation with Dagg Drummond across the Dearborn. The Diamond-D man had complimented John on the condition of his cattle, the site of his ranch house and the richness of his pasture land but all the time he spoke, despite the constant grin on his face, John felt threatened by the words. The more he thought about what Dagg had said the more sure he was that the Diamond-D intended having his land. He hadn't mentioned the conversation to Ellen. She, he knew, would dig in her heels and tell the Drummonds to go to hell if they came around trying to buy the land. She would rake up, once more, the history of how her parents had settled and cultivated this part of the territory before anyone else was here — including the Drummonds. This ranch was a testimony to her family's spirit and she would never leave it. John called this place home too, but only because he'd married Ellen. He'd drifted this way after the war, found work here as a cowboy and married the owner's daughter. He was content enough with his life and, until recently, had had no thought of moving elsewhere but if the Drummonds had their eyes on this land then perhaps it was time to start afresh somewhere else. No land was worth dying over. If the Drummonds were prepared to make a good offer, as they had done to Siggi Larrsen for his spread across the river, then he would give it proper consideration. He knew Ellen would oppose them but he also knew that every bit of land that, in the past, had been earmarked for adding to the Diamond-D empire, had been acquired. Some owners, like Siggi, had been prepared to do business, had accepted the offer and moved on. Others, smaller holdings north of Bridger Butte, spreads that the owners had been reluctant to sell, met with all manner of misfortunes. Cattle were rustled, horse herds run off and buildings caught fire. Suspicion and accusation were thrown in the direction of the Diamond-D but not supported with evidence and, when the banks threatened to foreclose on their mortgage, the struggling ranchers were left with no alternative other than to sell their ranch for a desultory sum. There had also been isolated instances of violence against some of those ranchers or members of their crew. Again, it was difficult to tie these incidents in with the offer for their land but rumour of Diamond-D involvement was rife. And there had been the dubious death of

Bart Lomax at the height of a bitter wrangle over his land with Luther Drummond. Few people believed it to be the riding accident officially recorded; Bart was a good horseman; the river crossing where his body was found was easy. The question of whether he fell on the rock that split open his skull or the rock fell on him was discussed in hushed tones in saloons and ranch houses across the territory. 'Luther Drummond,' John told Ethan, 'who owns the Diamond-D, is kingpin hereabouts. His word is law. Has been since long before I came to this territory and I'm not looking to have any trouble with him.'

His words nettled Ellen. 'Well he hasn't been in this territory any longer than my family and even if he has built something of an empire for himself he needn't think he's going to extend it by taking our land or by stopping us using the trail to Bridger Butte. That's public land. The trail's open to everyone.'

Ethan Brodie added his own comment. 'I wasn't looking for trouble when I rode across the river, but his men stole my horse and gear and I aim to get it all back.' He stood and headed for the door, coffee and salve left untouched on the table. The cuts and bruises on his face didn't bother him too much, his most pressing concern was the tightening skin below his shirt. He hadn't inspected those bruises, hadn't shown them to Ellen Hartley, but he knew they must cover the greater part of his midriff. They induced a sharp pain with every sharp movement and deep breath. He stopped in the doorway. 'I need to be underway,' he said to John Hartley. 'I'd be obliged if you'd provide that rifle and horse we'd agreed on.'

From a rack on the wall, John Hartley selected a Winchester which he placed in Ethan's hands as he passed to go outside. Ethan checked the mechanism then pushed some cartridges into the chamber. 'Thank you for your care,

Mrs Hartley,' he told Ellen. 'I'll have your horse back before nightfall.' With those words he left the ranch house and traced John Hartley's steps to the corral where the rancher was leading a big black horse to the hitching rail.

5

The stage robbers followed the wagon road south until they were out of sight of the stricken stagecoach then cut up into the high ground and circled back riding east then north until they were almost back on the trail to Bridger Butte. In a natural delve in the hillside, where the river swung in a long, lazy loop, they stopped, dismounted, pulled off their blankets and tethered the horses.

For Chad Trelawney, the outlaw who had fought the now dead passenger, the hard ride had been something of an ordeal. Groggy at the outset from the blows he'd taken, the hard ride had left him with blurred vision and pains in the head which came with frightening intensity. He slumped beside a tree on the bank of the river, grateful for the coldness of the running water in which

he dipped his neckerchief. He dabbed it against the bruises and cuts on his face and finally held it over his eyes to try to free himself of the nausea caused by the coloured flashes that had beset him since stepping down from the saddle.

If Chad expected sympathy or assistance from his cohorts, it was in short supply. Charlie Tyson and Lou Petersen were more concerned about the money they'd taken from the strong box and the passengers. Chad could hear their voices but couldn't summon up sufficient concentration to decipher the words. For the moment all he cared about was clearing his head so that he would be well enough to complete the ride back to the bunk-house.

When they'd amassed the paper money that had been in the strong-box with the pocket contents of the three passengers the total was a little over five hundred dollars. 'Little more than a hundred each,' said Lou.

'You can keep my share,' said Dagg

Drummond. 'This is what I was after.' He held up the linen belt that had been around the dead passenger's waist. 'This is Drummond money. Siggi Larrsen was a fool if he thought he was leaving the territory with this.'

'How much is in there?' Lou asked.

'None of your business,' snapped Dagg. 'Like I said, this is Drummond money. You've done OK with the rest.'

Lou's retort made it clear he didn't share Dagg's opinion. 'Five hundred and thirty dollars between three of us. Ain't exactly a fortune.'

'It's six months' pay for five minutes' work,' snarled Dagg. 'That seems like adequate payment to me.'

'Nothing more than a good table stake in the Red Feathers,' grumbled Lou.

Charlie chuckled, a mean, low sound. He jerked his head in Chad's direction. 'Might not even cover his doctor bill.'

Grabbing the opportunity to end the conversation with Lou, Dagg turned his attention to Chad. 'What were you doing letting Larrsen beat up on you like that?'

Chad lifted the damp cloth from his eyes, tried to focus on Dagg. Through the persistent jags of pain, his mind had been trying to come to terms with a not dissimilar question, only he was wondering why his companions had allowed Larrsen to attack him. If Dagg had intended killing the big Swede why had he not done so before he'd belaboured Chad with a rock. There had been three of them watching; any one of them could have intervened and saved him from Larrsen's attack. If the pain in his head hadn't been enough for him to handle he would have thrown the question back at Dagg Drummond. Instead, as white pain lanced through his brain, he was only capable of an almost indiscernible mumble 'He took me by surprise.'

'Took you by surprise,' scoffed Dagg. 'If I hadn't been there to help he would have killed you.'

Chad was well enough aware of that

and didn't appreciate Dagg rubbing it in. He lowered his neckerchief once more into the stream then draped the soaking cloth over his face. Dagg turned away, his expression part sneer and part celebration at the other man's discomfort. 'I'm riding for Billings,' he announced. 'Gotta put this into a bank.' He hefted the linen belt in his hands but no one was in any doubt as to what he referred to. 'You three had better get back on the range to alibi yourselves. Get up on the north pastures and stay there. I'll join you sometime tomorrow. Don't go into Bridger Butte. I don't want you gambling big and raising suspicion. And you,' he called back to Chad, 'you'd better not go into town until your face heals.' When no one responded, Dagg went across to the horses. 'I'm taking your horse, Chad. This other is too easily identified. Wouldn't do for someone on the stagecoach to recognize it when they get to Billings.'

Again no one spoke. Dagg was the

ranch owner's son and they were all riding Diamond-D horses. They really didn't have any say in the matter. Charlie, who had bitten off a lump of chewing tobacco when he'd first dismounted, ejected a long stream of red spittle towards the river but made no other movement until Dagg had ridden up out of the delve and could be seen in stark outline galloping along the crest of the high ground. 'Don't suppose the dumb critters on the north pasture will miss us. Build a fire up, Lou. I'll brew some coffee. Reckon Chad would appreciate resting here a while.'

* * *

The well-schooled, rangy gelding needed little more guidance than to be pointed in the right direction as it tackled the hill trail. Upon its back sat Dagg Drummond, as confident at that moment as he was ever likely to be with a horse under him. This had nothing to do with his horsemanship or the quality of the horse itself, merely a by-product of his upbringing. He had been raised like a prince, his accession to the throne of the Diamond-D governed only by time. In this domain his words and deeds were sacrosanct, above challenge from all but his father. His instructions had to be carried out without question, an obedience which he expected not only from the hired hands but the dumb beasts, too. Unnatural as such a belief might be, and Dagg would certainly deny owning it, it was the inner certainty that everything in that area of Montana was there for his benefit that provided his inner assurance. Just as surely as he expected any of the ranch-hands to carry out his instructions so he was convinced that any Diamond-D reared mount would carry him safely to his destination. Hence his anger at the beast with the broken leg. It had failed him. That was unacceptable.

Such unreasonable expectations

served to highlight Dagg's lack of affinity with livestock, a lack, sadly, which extended to people. Although he ordered and they obeyed, he was never smart enough to realize he was tolerated without respect. Every experienced hand at the Diamond-D knew that Dagg Drummond hadn't the ability to run the ranch. Often, work done under Dagg's instruction was re-done or abandoned altogether when it came to the attention of Gus Hardin, the foreman. But this was Luther Drummond's empire and his son was the natural successor so no one disobeyed Dagg. Eventually, most hands, unwilling to waste their energy on worthless jobs and to suffer the moodiness of the oft thwarted Dagg, sought out Gus Hardin when tasks were being allotted. Only those whose association with Dagg seemed more personal rode out with him each morning. They were the three he had left at the river and they clung to Dagg in the expectation that their current loyalty would reap dividends when he inherited the ranch.

Despite the advantages he enjoyed as the son of Luther Drummond, Dagg's general demeanour was one of surliness, due entirely to his distaste for the future life expected of him. His only happiness seemed to stem from displaying his power to other people, enjoying their suffering especially if it led to his gain. Although he'd been raised with the expectation of controlling one of Montana's largest cattle spreads, such a prospect held little thrill for him. He hated ranch life. Dust and cows were something to avoid but, until recently, no other life had seemed possible for him. He'd listened to his father's plans for a bigger ranch and bigger herds, his legacy to his son. Luther had discussed with him all aspects of ranching, taking for granted Dagg's desire to succeed him. Apart from Dagg's need for a wife, no other subject was ever discussed, which led to Dagg seeking company away from the ranch, at the gambling tables and bedrooms of the Drover's Rope and Red Feathers.

Then, one night, he met Jethro Rhodes, a man with a camera recording the land and people of the Dakotas, Wyoming and Montana. Caught up in Jethro's enthusiasm for the collection of photographs he'd taken at the lumber camp outside Enterprise, Dagg invited him to the Diamond-D. Three days of listening to Jethro's explanations for choosing one site instead of another and the technical requirements for obtaining the best results were enough to convince Dagg that travelling with a camera was the life for him.

Then came winter and all other matters were abandoned in the battle to save cattle and when spring arrived the losses were calculated and re-building stock levels became the priority. For a while, Luther's land extension plans had proved a source of amusement to Dagg, allowing him to exert pressure on unwilling sellers to drive them from their homesteads. Greater pressure than his father knew; pressure that had led to casualties. Men, livestock and property had suffered but no one openly mentioned the name Drummond in connection with those casualties. In Dagg's opinion, nothing else mattered to his father except building the empire he hoped to pass on to his son but when copies of Jethro's photographs arrived Dagg knew it was an empire he didn't want.

Now, as he reached the ridge, he touched the saddlebag which was stuffed with the full linen money belt. Forty thousand dollars, he estimated, enough to set him up in business and make him independent of his father. The fact that he had killed two men to get that money held no significance. He hadn't spared a thought for either of them since leaving Gunner Pass. This land was Drummond land and everything upon it, subject to the forebearance of the Drummonds.

★   ★   ★

When Dagg Drummond reached the summit of the climb up from the river making himself visible to the men he'd left behind, another pair of eyes spotted him and recognized his thickset body shape and the light coloured shirt he wore. Ethan Brodie hadn't pushed along at any great haste. The horse he'd borrowed from John Hartley was a sound beast, well capable of sustaining a brisk pace for several miles, but Ethan was a stranger to the territory and had no idea where his quarry was headed. Furthermore, because he was sticking to the recognized trail, it was impossible to identify either individual or recent tracks. So he'd ridden steadily, keeping a lookout to right and left, along the skyline and down the slopes to the river.

When Dagg first emerged into view, Ethan's first instinct was to give chase. There was no doubt in his mind that this was the man who had pounded him with fists and rifle butt and who had ordered his humiliation by having him strung between two trees. But common sense checked his desire for revenge. Recovering his horse was his first object and that man he could see was astride a different cayuse. Which · meant, he reasoned, that one of the other men had it and that his best chance of finding them was to follow the man's back trail.

Gently he urged forward his borrowed horse, moving at a slow, easy walk, hoping no creak of leather or the jangle of bridle or stirrup would betray his whereabouts. He followed the tracks the man had cut through the cypress and willows and when he could hear the rushing of the water in the stream he dismounted. Ethan pulled the rifle from its saddle boot and edged forward. From the tree line he could see two men. One, who he recognized from earlier in the day, was bent over a collection of twigs and seemed to have a fire going. The second — the one Ethan had heard called Charlie — was at the river bank, scooping water into a black coffee pot. If Charlie hadn't paused on his way back to where the fire was leaping into life, Ethan probably wouldn't have seen the third man who was slumped on the ground beneath one of the willow trees. So still and awkward did he lie that Ethan had mistaken him for a log. Even though Charlie was talking to the man there was no sign of any response.

Ethan let Charlie get all the way back to the fire before stepping into the clearing. That way, he had the two active men close together so they were easier to cover. He ratcheted the rifle's mechanism which had the double function of ensuring there was a bullet in the chamber and, with its unmistakable sound, warned the others not to reach for their own weapons.

'You,' said Charlie who still held the coffee pot in his right hand.

Lou Petersen, who was kneeling by the fire and had his back to Ethan, began to rise.

'Slowly,' said Ethan, 'and lift your hands above your head.' Lou threw a glance over his shoulder and, recognizing Ethan, expressed his surprise. 'How did you get here?'

'That's not important,' Ethan replied. 'Just unfasten your gunbelt. With your left hand. Now, let it drop and walk over there.' He indicated the river-bank. 'Keep going until I tell you to stop.' Lou remained motionless, matching Ethan's unblinking gaze with a stare that flashed incredulity, that he found amusement in Ethan's behaviour, that seeking revenge for what happened earlier was a lost cause, that the next time they met he would kill him. 'Do it,' ordered Ethan. 'I'd as soon put a bullet in you as not.' Lou grinned, a display of bravado. Ethan fired, the bullet kicking up dirt between Lou's feet. When he indicated with the rifle Lou walked slowly to the river-bank and stopped. 'I didn't tell you to stop,' shouted Ethan. 'Keep going until I do.'

Lou looked back over his shoulder and began to open his mouth in protest. Ethan fired again, the bullet almost hitting Lou's right foot. He stepped into the water and kept going. The river wasn't as deep as Ethan hoped. Even in the middle when he told Lou to stop, it wasn't knee high. 'Now you,' he told Charlie.

Charlie followed suit. Ethan made him hold the coffee pot in his right hand while he unfastened his gunbelt with his left. He made him walk six paces towards the river before telling him to put down the coffee pot. 'What's the matter with him?' Ethan indicated Chad.

'He's sick.'

'Then you'll have to take off his gunbelt and help him to stand over there.' He pointed to the middle of the river where Lou still stood with his hands in the air. Charlie thought about protesting but Ethan levered his weapon again to emphasize the fact that he wouldn't stand for any delay. When Charlie began to kneel in front of Chad, Ethan issued another order. 'Get to the other side of him. I want to see what you're doing. I'll drill you if either of you do anything silly.' Charlie scowled but removed Chad's gunbelt and threw it towards the fire. Chad was conscious, and lying still had a beneficial effect. Although there was still pain, it was less severe and the flashing lights had ceased. With Charlie's assistance he waded to the middle of the river.

Ethan gathered up the gunbelts. Attached to one of them, the one belonging to the tall, thin fellow, he noticed a trinket. On examination, he discovered it to be a silver disc. An eagle's head was etched on one face. It hung on a thong of thick, black cord which was carefully entwined around the buckle of the cartridge belt. He carried the three gunbelts across where the horses were tethered and hooked them over the saddle horns of the two Diamond-D horses. Then he ran an experienced eye over his own horse to ensure it hadn't suffered any injury while it had been away from him. He gathered the lead reins of all three animals and headed for the tree line.

Lou shouted. 'Where are you going with our horses.'

'This one is mine,' Ethan told him. 'I'll leave the others along the trail.'

'Mister, you don't know what trouble you're making for yourself. This is Diamond-D country and those are Diamond-D horses.'

'This isn't Diamond-D land,' Ethan shouted back, 'and I've told you the horses will be somewhere towards Bridger Butte.'

'May not be Diamond-D land,' Charlie called, 'but Luther Drummond stills calls the shots here. You made a big mistake picking an argument with Luther Drummond.'

'I've got no argument with Luther Drummond. My argument was with you when you beat me up and stole my horse. Now that I've got my horse I'll continue my journey, but stay out of my way. I haven't forgotten what you did to me and I won't be as tolerant again.'

Further shouts of anger followed him as he disappeared among the trees. He jumped into the saddle of the waiting Hartley horse and began the climb up to the high ground and the trail to Bridger Butte.

He led the three horses for almost five miles before pulling up on a stretch of open pasture which had an easy slope down to the river. Before setting loose the two horses which bore the Diamond-D brand, Ethan removed their bridles and tied them to the saddles. This left the animals free to forage while they waited for their owners to catch up.

Shortly after, Ethan arrived once more at the Hartley spread. He called to the house but got no reply. He unsaddled the borrowed horse and rubbed it down with a handful of straw before allowing it to drink from the trough by the corral. Then he turned it in with the rest of John Hartley's string, threw the saddle over the top pole of the corral and took the rifle up to the ranch house. He called to the house again and knocked on the door but no one answered. So he went inside and hung the rifle back on the wall rack.

Outside again, he climbed once more into his own saddle. Another hour, he told the weary horse, and they would be in Bridger Butte. They would both enjoy a rest when they got there.

6

Ensuring passengers reached their destination as swiftly as possible was the number one priority of Friars Stage Line, the company who ran the Montana stage routes, so, in the event of a hold-up, it was usual for the driver to proceed with all urgency to the next stop down the line. On this occasion, however, following the hold-up at Gunner Pass, Jonas 'Bullwhip' Saxon, the stagecoach driver, chose to return to Enterprise, his decision influenced by several factors. First, they were only a handful of miles from Enterprise while proceeding to Billings meant a journey of several hours with no other large settlement in between. Bullwhip reckoned that the sooner he reported the incident to a lawman the greater chance there was that the outlaws would be traced and caught. In addition, it was a long journey to make without a shotgun guard and he wasn't convinced that, in any future emergency, the two remaining passengers would be of any assistance to him. On top of that, Siggi Larrsen, the dead passenger, and Joe Dumbril, the guard, were Bridger Butte men. Joe, for certain, had family there. His daughter would want him buried in the town cemetery.

Less than an hour after the robbery the stagecoach arrived back in Enterprise, the horses and wheels kicking up a small storm of dust and stones as it raced between the two lines of wood-framed buildings that constituted the town's main street. Bullwhip hauled on the leather strings, bringing the team to an abrupt halt outside the Bitterroot Star, an establishment which was little better than a saloon and bawdy house but which was the only place that had accommodation for travellers and which held the town's franchise for the stage line.

The unexpected and reckless return of the stagecoach drew a cluster of curious townsfolk to the boardwalk outside the Bitterroot Star. When the proprietor, John Carswell, known as Turkey, stepped outside, Bullwhip broadcast the news. 'We were held up at Gunner Pass. Four of them. They killed Joe Dumbril and Siggi Larrsen. Mr Carswell, if you fix it so I've got someone up on the box with me, I'll make the run tomorrow. Horses aren't up to another journey today.'

Carswell announced to the crowd that the coach would leave next day four hours ahead of its usual noon start. In line with the terms of his franchise, he offered overnight accommodation in the Bitterroot Star to the returning passengers but, as both were citizens of Enterprise, the rooms were not required. Jed Cassidy indeed, he who had been travelling to his brother's funeral, declared that his trip was no longer necessary. 'The funeral will be over before I reach Billings,' he grumbled. 'All I want from Friar's Stage Line is a full refund of my fare and restitution of the money I was carrying.' His voice was full of complaint but carried little conviction. Recently, misfortune had been his regular companion so, although he thought it right that the stage line should pay his losses, he had little expectation of seeing the money.

Turkey Carswell, unwilling to conduct a financial discussion on the street, wrapped an arm around Jed's shoulder and led him inside the Bitterroot Star while issuing soothing words that he would send a telegram to the headquarters in Great Falls asking for immediate authorization to fulfil all claims. He had no idea what Friar's reaction would be to such a request but once he'd sent the telegram the matter was out of his hands. His sympathy for Jed Cassidy need know no bounds. Whoever was going to end up out of pocket over the hold-up, it wasn't going to be him.

It was because of the lumber camp

that Enterprise had come into being. Initially, Bridger Butte had been the location of its operational base but the expansion of the project brought in more men and a need for stores and stockyards dedicated to the use of the loggers. These were sited higher up the slopes but close to an old trading trail which was soon developed into a wagon road. It wasn't long before a saloon was established to service the needs of the off-duty workmen, and several houses were erected to replace the canvas shelters that had first housed the timberjacks. Over the months, the settlement grew, and disputes became more prevalent, but they were the sort of disputes that arose in any male dominated community, the resolution of which usually began by rolling up shirt sleeves and ended by applying liniment to cuts and bruises. But the settlement never grew big enough nor the disputes violent enough to need an appointed law officer.

The sheriff of Bridger Butte was the

nearest lawman and it was to him that Bullwhip Saxon determined he would report the events at Gunner Pass. With the help of a couple of bystanders he had the bodies of Joe Dumbril and Siggi Larrsen transferred from the stagecoach to the flat bed of a buckboard. With a two horse team he set out for Bridger Butte and arrived there when the shadows were at their longest and the red sun had begun its dip behind the mountains.

News of Bullwhip's cargo spread along Drover Street, Bridger Butte's main thoroughfare, quicker than water over the Dearborn Falls in the springtime thaw. He hauled the team to a halt outside the office of Sheriff Bob Cotton and stayed on the driving board until the lawman stepped out on to the boardwalk. A couple of townsmen lifted the heavy canvas sheet to discover the identities of the bodies. The names were told, repeated among those approaching the buckboard and spread to those loitering outside the stores and saloons along the street.

'How did it happen?' someone asked Bullwhip.

'Who did it?' another wanted to know, but Bullwhip remained silent until Bob Cotton had looked at the bodies for himself.

'Stagecoach was held up on the way to Billings,' Bullwhip began. 'Four masked men stopped us at Gunner Pass. Murdered Joe Dumbril for protesting. Didn't even have a gun in his hand. The leader shot him in cold blood.' Among the crowd there were angry mutterings. Joe Dumbril had been a popular man in the town. A lot of heads turned towards the sheriff to see what action he proposed to take. 'As for the other fellow,' continued Bullwhip, 'they killed him when he tried to hang on to his money. Did a fair bit of damage to one of the outlaws before the leader plugged him.'

'Siggi Larrsen,' the sheriff spoke the dead man's name reflectively. 'Just sold his ranch to Luther Drummond. Could be he was carrying a lot of money with him.'

'Sure was,' remarked Bullwhip. 'Carrying it in a money belt under his shirt, and if you want my opinion, sheriff, those road agents knew what Siggi was carrying. The leader had Siggi's valise searched. Just Siggi's. And when there was no money found in that, they hit on the idea that he was wearing a money belt. That's when Siggi fought back. Near enough hammered the daylights out of one of the men. Hit him a couple of times with a rock. That man won't be moving easily for a few days.'

Above the mumbling and comments of the crowd pleased to know that Siggi Larrsen had inflicted some pain on his killers, Bob Cotton threw another question at Bullwhip. 'Any idea who they were?'

Bullwhip rubbed his jaw and shook his head. 'Only that they knew that Siggi was carrying a lot of money.'

'A lot of people knew that,' said Bob Cotton. 'Selling out to the Diamond-D wasn't exactly a secret. Nor was the fact that he was leaving town today.'

'There was one other thing, sheriff. The leader was riding a handsome horse. Unmistakable. Red as a fox on chest and flanks but white as snow at the rear. Mane and tail were white, too. Never before seen a horse with such colouring.'

The description of the horse spread among those congregated but no one could claim any knowledge of it. Bob Cotton ordered some of the men to take the bodies to the undertaker's parlour and a woman standing nearby volunteered to get word to Joe's daughter.

'You gonna organize a posse, sheriff?' asked Bullwhip. 'I brung the news as quickly as I could so we could get after them today.'

Sheriff Cotton looked up at the reddening sky. 'Too late now, Bullwhip. By the time I get a group of men deputized, saddled up and out to Gunner Pass, the daylight will be gone.

I'll select some men tonight and we'll set out at first light tomorrow.'

This didn't satisfy Bullwhip who had hoped to set out with the posse himself. Joe Dumbril had been a good friend. The thought that he might not be instrumental in catching his killer didn't sit easily with him. He searched his mind for an argument that would change Bob Cotton's plan but common sense told him that the sheriff was right; within an hour it would be too dark to see any trail. He murmured one last comment to the sheriff, a piece of information that had forced its way into his consciousness, one final recollection even though he knew its value was nil. 'They headed south when they left us,' he said. 'Riding towards Billings.'

Bob Cotton voiced the argument that made Bullwhip's information valueless. 'But once out of sight they could have gone up into the high ground and then to any corner of the state.'

If a voice hadn't risen from the crowd at the moment, Bullwhip would have been left with little choice but to turn the buckboard round and, down-hearted, head back to Enterprise. But, heeding the cry, 'Look at this,' he turned like everyone else in the street to look in the direction that the man pointed. Heading along Drover Street, its neck outstretched with weariness, came a horse that exactly matched the description that Bullwhip had recently given. A shock of white mane fell forward over its red face, and upon its back a rider who, if not asleep in the saddle, was slumped forward in obvious physical discomfort.

As horse and rider drew closer to the group outside the sheriff's office, Bullwhip peered closely at them. 'Goshamighty,' he declared, 'that's him. No mistaking that horse, sheriff. That's the one the leader rode. Pulled right out in front of us as we came down the hill. That's him, all right. That's the man who killed Joe and Siggi.'

Those final few words were enough to goad the gathered citizens into

action. Building a comm...
territory could only ...
acting together, adhe...
for peaceful coexistenc...
ing and honouring ...
property and boundaries. ...
there were men who would ...
the wild side, would take wha...
wanted and live off another n...
labour. Cattle rustlers, horse thie...
and road agents were the bane of the
lives of those people who were trying
to bring civilization to the frontier
land. When caught, the treatment of
those who lived outside the law was
seldom lenient. Often, with no recognized lawman or jail cell within a day's
journey, their trial, sentencing and
execution was undertaken in minutes
— lynched from the nearest tree. And
such was the intention of the
townsmen of Bridger Butte who, with
growing tumult, advanced on the
stranger on the distinctive horse.

Stirred from his lethargy by the
commotion, Ethan Brodie was helpless

the numerous hands that
d at his arms and legs, pulling
to one side of his horse and then
other before crashing to the dry,
ed street with a body aching thud.
s shouts of protest were ignored, and
hough some men were trying to pull
him to his feet others were taking full
advantage of his helplessness and
delivering sly punches to whatever part
of him they could reach. Most of the
punches carried no real power, the
density of the throng preventing any
opportunity for a full swing of the arm,
but those which landed on those areas
of Ethan's body which had suffered the
greatest, earlier punishment, made him
wince and gasp for breath.

Through the stabs of pain and above
the general hubbub he could hear clear
shouts. 'Get a rope!' 'String him up!'
'Killer!' 'Hanging's too good for what
he done.' Ethan tried to struggle but his
arms were tightly held. Soon a loop was
tossed over his shoulders fastening his
arms to his side even more securely. He

tried to question the nearest man but couldn't make himself heard or understood above the noise of the mob. He felt himself being propelled along the street to where a noose had been thrown over an extended angle beam of a corner building. He tried to dig his heels into the dirt of the street but his resistance went unnoticed as he was scuttled towards the makeshift scaffold.

Then a shot rang out. And another, stilling the crowd, turning heads back to the spot where Ethan had been dragged from his horse. 'Bring that man back,' yelled Bob Cotton.

'He killed Joe Dumbril,' shouted the man nearest Ethan. 'And Siggi Larrsen.'

'That may be true,' the sheriff announced, 'but we've got to prove it.'

'What more proof do you want, sheriff,' another voiced asked, this a young man with pale skin and a well shaped moustache. 'Bullwhip identified him and he was there.'

'Seems I recall Bullwhip saying that

the men were masked,' replied Bob Cotton. 'I want to hear that fella's story so bring him back to my office. Now.' He brandished his six-gun in the general direction of the crowd but they were reluctant to release their captive.

'Bullwhip also described that horse before it came to town. There cain't be two like it.'

While that man argued with Bob Cotton, another was examining the pack behind Ethan's saddle. He pulled off a roll of grey cloth and unrolled it showing the hole that had been cut in the middle.

Bullwhip yelped. 'Thet's what they wore. All of them hid under a blanket like that and had a neckerchief up to their eyes. Yep, sheriff. He's surely one of them.' The mob roared again and would have dragged Ethan to his doom but another gunshot roared out, this time the deeper boom of a shotgun which stilled the townsmen again. When they looked back to the place where Bob Cotton stood they saw he had company. A man stood either side of the sheriff, each with a deputy star on his chest and a shotgun in his hands. Smoke spiralled lazily from one.

'Now I ain't gonna tell you again,' said the sheriff. 'Bring that man back to my office.'

'Ain't Bullwhip's identification evidence enough of his guilt, Sheriff?'

'Perhaps so, but Bullwhip also told us there were four of them involved in the hold-up. I want that man to tell me the names of the other three and where I can find them.' That argument carried the necessary weight to get the response the sheriff wanted from the citizens. Reluctantly and with a grumbling undercurrent, they brought Ethan back to the boardwalk outside the sheriff's office. 'What's your name?'

'Ethan Brodie. I don't know what this is all about, Sheriff, but I didn't kill anyone.'

7

Inside the sheriff's office, Bob Cotton sat in the seat behind his desk while the two deputies each stood by a window watching the still restless activity outside. Ethan, the rope removed from around his arms and his pistol long since removed from its holster by he knew not whom, sat in a chair in the middle of the room. He rubbed where the friction of the rope had burned his skin. The lawman spoke to him. 'So you didn't kill anyone,' he said, his tone flat, carrying neither an edge of anger nor belief in Ethan's innocence. 'I suppose you're going to tell me you weren't involved in a stage robbery either.'

'That's right,' said Ethan. 'I wasn't.'

Bob Cotton shook his head slowly, a wry smile on his face, a smile which demonstrated the sheriff's disbelief more emphatically than any words he might have uttered. A smile that promised to sweep away whatever alibi Ethan offered as surely as a spring flood on the Missouri would wash away a beaver's dam. 'And I suppose you're going to deny that horse you rode into town on is yours, too.'

'No. The horse is mine.'

'Kinda distinctive, isn't he?'

Ethan had to agree. 'He is.'

'No one around here has ever seen a horse with such marking before so it would be a heck of a coincidence if two turned up on the same day. Wouldn't you agree?' He paused long enough for Ethan to nod his head. 'Now Bullwhip out there,' Bob Cotton continued, 'he was the driver of the stage that was robbed. Got a good eye for detail, has Bullwhip, and seeing how Joe Dumbril, the shotgun guard who was killed, was Bullwhip's friend, you can be sure he remembers every little thing about the robbery. He identified that horse you rode in on without hesitation. Described it so well that every man in town recognized it as soon as you hit Drover Street.'

Ethan looked at the glint in the soft-spoken sheriff's eyes and assessed him as a wily man. 'The horse is mine,' he told the lawman again, 'but earlier today he was stolen from me.'

Bob Cotton sat back in his chair, his expression reflecting the possibility of a truth he'd never suspected. 'Stolen, eh! OK, let's hear your story. You think you've got something to say that will prove you were somewhere else when the coach was robbed at Gunner Pass then spit it out.' If Ethan thought Bob Cotton proposed listening to him with an open mind, his follow up remark shattered the illusion. 'After that I want you to tell me who the other three men were and where they are now.'

The picture of three men standing knee deep in the river six or seven miles from the Hartley ranch flashed into Ethan's mind. For an instant he considered revealing their predicament to the sheriff. It could be that they hadn't yet recovered their horses and were still trudging the hill trail to where he'd left them. Unarmed, as they were, a posse would round them up without conflict. But immediately he put that thought aside, if those men had reached their horses they could be anywhere now. Ethan's first priority was to prove his innocence, the key to which was the testimony of John and Ellen Hartley. So he began his story from his first visit to the Hartley ranch.

When Ethan recounted the episode across the river, Bob Cotton's attitude changed. He pressed Ethan for descriptions of the four men and when he was done the silence in the room hung as heavy as a wet horse blanket on a sapling bough. The deputies had ceased their street vigil, their attention captured by Ethan's commentary. Meaningful looks were exchanged with each other and the sheriff.

'Do you recognize these men?' Ethan asked.

Sheriff Cotton was noncommittal.

'Those descriptions could fit a lot of people,' he said.

'Sure they could,' said Ethan, 'but do they fit the description of any Diamond-D riders? They threw that brand name around like it gave them impunity from the law.'

Bob Cotton didn't respond to that comment, instead he asked Ethan how he'd got away.

'Mrs Hartley came looking for me. She couldn't understand why my horse was heading south with a different rider shortly after she'd watched me heading towards the river and Bridger Butte.' Bob Cotton sat silently rubbing his jaw while the rest of the tale unfolded. 'You can verify my story with the Hartleys,' Ethan told him, 'and there's a dead horse just above the river which probably has the brand of the Diamond-D on its rump.'

Mention of John and Ellen Hartley clearly put a dent in Sheriff Cotton's scepticism. Local people who could provide an alibi was an unexpected turn of events and one which couldn't be ignored. He told Casey Drew, one of the deputies, to bring the stagecoach driver inside. 'Bullwhip,' he said, 'I want you to take a good look at this man and tell me just how sure you are he's one of those that stopped the coach.'

Bullwhip shuffled, a movement full of determination and intent, his eyes flashing a message at Ethan that he wanted retribution for the death of his partner and the passenger and that he wasn't the sort of lily-livered citizen who would shy away from pointing his finger at whoever he believed to be responsible. He looked Ethan over, grumbled under his breath then looked around the room for a spittoon in which he could fire his next length of baccy juice. By the time he found it and used it the fire of revenge that had animated his features and movement had been doused with doubt. 'That was the horse,' he declared, as though his certainty on that point ought to satisfy Bob Cotton.

'But the man,' said the Sheriff, 'is there anything about him that you can identify?'

Bullwhip shuffled again, this time it was a delaying tactic, not wanting to say no but not able to say yes. Bob Cotton prompted him again. 'Anything, Bullwhip?'

'Like I told you earlier,' the driver said, 'they were covered with blankets and didn't show much of their faces. Perhaps if he moved about.'

Ethan was told to stand and walk around the office. The deputies kept their weapons pointed at him, a warning not to try to make a dash for the door. Bullwhip looked him up and down, his mouth twisting in consternation. 'He's too tall,' he said eventually. 'The guy that killed Siggi Larrsen was shorter and he was wearing a black hat. No one was wearing a hat like that one. Haven't seen one of those high-domes since my days along the Pecos.'

'Are you telling me he wasn't one of the robbers?' Bob Cotton asked.

'I don't know what I'm telling you,' growled Bullwhip, 'but that horse out there was definitely involved.'

'Can't arrest the horse,' Bob said, his tone holding more disappointment than humour.

'What about me?' Ethan asked. 'Am I free to go?'

'Not yet,' said the sheriff. 'Casey, put him in a cell and guard him while me an' Ben check out his story. If John and Ellen Hartley confirm what he's told us we'll head on towards Gunner Pass and hope to catch those men afoot.'

Casey Drew motioned with his rifle for Ethan to head towards the cells but before he'd taken a couple of steps the street door was flung wide open with an abruptness which startled those inside the jailhouse. The door swung back as far as it could go, colliding with a low chest of drawers that stood against the wall, striking it so violently that the resulting noise suggested the place was being stormed by a determined lynch mob. The lawmen reacted, turning to

101

face the suspected onslaught and reaching for their guns, but when their initial confusion was resolved they saw that only one person stood in the doorway.

She was a slight girl. Her fair hair showed only in stray wisps that had escaped from beneath the brown suede hat that sat firmly on her head. She wore a red calico shirt of which only the top button was unfastened and her trousers were loose fitting and fringed and tailored from soft doeskin. There was blood on her hands and it stained the cuffs of her shirt and she held a rifle in a manner which proclaimed she knew how to use it. There were trails on her cheeks where tears had cut through the dust and the rims of her eyes were red where they'd been rubbed dry. As she advanced into the room her attention never wavered from Ethan. She walked stiffly, unnaturally, the demeanour of one who has vowed an undertaking and won't be dissuaded from her cause. Even so, there was a tremble of emotion in her voice when she spoke. 'Is this the man they say killed my father?'

Bob Cotton stepped forward. 'Claire,' he said, holding out his hands, hoping to take the rifle from her.

Ignoring the sheriff, she stepped closer to his prisoner and spoke his name. 'Ethan Brodie?' she asked.

Ethan nodded. He examined her face. Despite her struggle to prevent the tears that welled in her eyes from overflowing and despite the anger and distress that were presently written in her features, he could see that she was very pretty.

'This man didn't kill my father,' she said and took her left hand from the rifle so that she could wipe the sleeve over her face.

Bob Cotton looked from her to Ethan then back to Claire Dumbril. 'Do you know this man, Claire?'

It was another voice that answered. Another female voice. This girl, dressed soberly in a plain grey dress with a blue fabric belt and carrying a matching blue bonnet, had arrived unobserved behind Claire. 'I do,' she said. 'He's my brother.'

Irene Claymore and her husband James had arrived in Bridger Butte three years earlier. James Claymore was an attorney and although, at first, the cattlemen had had little need for his services, the more businesslike timber company had welcomed him from day one. Increasingly, the ranchers had accepted the need for legal representation and James Claymore's position in the community had risen accordingly. While her husband's reputation and wealth was growing, Irene had dedicated herself to founding a school for the children of the area. She had begun by holding a class each morning in the unlikely surroundings of the stockroom of the Drover's Rope, the biggest saloon in Bridger Butte, but that had soon proved unsuitable because of interruptions from the barman who needed constant access to supplies, and because its size was insufficient as the number of pupils increased. So, for a while, they gathered in a barn on Joe Dumbril's land but its location was inconvenient and a temporary solution was a room added on to the back of her husband's office while she made plans with the town council to have a permanent school built. Donations and offers had not been in short supply and the building, on the western edge of town, would soon be completed. So, like her husband, Irene Claymore was a noted figure in Bridger Butte.

'Your brother, Mrs Claymore?'

'Yes, Sheriff. I haven't seen him for six years but I got a letter a few days ago to tell me he was going to come a visiting. He can't have had anything to do with the stagecoach robbery.'

Bob Cotton was pretty sure she was right. Bullwhip had been quite adamant that the robbers had been aware of the money Siggi Larrsen had been carrying and that pointed to the felons being local men. Indeed, it was only the horse that put Ethan Brodie under suspicion and if his story stood up to scrutiny then there was no reason to hold him. 'I'm heading out now to the Hartley spread,' he told Irene Claymore. 'If his story checks out then he'll be free to go.'

'You're going to put him in the cells?'

'Got to. For his own safety as much as anything else. Two good men were murdered today. Without positive proof that your brother isn't the killer he might not be too safe around town.'

Claire Dumbril spoke. 'But I know he didn't do it and my father was one of the men killed.'

'Then you can play an important part in keeping a lid on things if you spread that around, and you,' he turned to Bullwhip, 'can do likewise by spreading it around that Brodie here doesn't match your memory of the robbers.' Bullwhip grumbled under his breath but it was without any real animosity.

Irene Claymore tried again. 'Can't you release Ethan into our custody? My husband will stand surety for him, Sheriff.'

Bob Cotton shifted from foot to foot. 'In other circumstances I might do that, Mrs Claymore, but armed robbery is different. I'm sure your husband will understand. But I'll speak to the Hartleys as soon as I can. Your brother might only be here for a couple of hours. You can bring him something to eat. By the time he's finished a meal I could be letting him go.'

That seemed to be the best Irene could hope for and she could only stand by as her brother was locked away in one of the cells at the back of the office.

'You will get the men who killed my father, won't you?' Claire Dumbril inquired of Sheriff Cotton.

'That's our intention, Claire. Now we've got to get out towards Gunner Pass before it gets too dark to see anything.'

But progress was to prove less hasty than the lawman intended. Before he reached the door it burst open again and John Hartley, flustered, hot and dusty from a furious ride stood in the doorway. His voice was loud, on the edge of panic. 'My wife, Ellen,' he said. 'She's missing.'

Ben Blackett, the other deputy, pulled out a seat and ushered the rancher towards it while Bob Cotton spoke in a placating manner. 'Sit down, John. What do you mean, missing?'

'She's gone. There was a stranger at the ranch today. I think he came back and kidnapped her.'

'Kidnapped? Take it easy, John. Tell me everything from the beginning. The stranger's name, do you know it?'

'Called himself Ethan Brodie. He's run off with my wife.'

Bob Cotton turned to the cells where Ethan stood listening, gripping iron bars. 'Ethan Brodie hasn't run off anywhere,' he told John Hartley and indicated with his head towards the back of the room.

John Hartley jumped up, tipping the chair to the floor, and rushed across to the cell where Ethan was imprisoned. 'What have you done to her?' he yelled. 'Where's Ellen?'

'I haven't done anything to her,' protested Ethan. 'I haven't seen her since she fixed my wounds and I left to get my horse back.' He agreed that he'd been back to the Hartley ranch to return the horse and gun he'd borrowed but told John that his wife had not been there.

John Hartley wasn't easily appeased. His anger and worry spilled out in a torrent of words and sentences which, the sheriff thought, if picked over carefully, probably contained sufficient facts to concur with what Ethan Brodie had told him. However, John Hartley's anger was too great to allow him to confirm Ethan's story so Bob Cotton decided he had to stay in jail until the disappearance of Ellen Hartley was explained.

8

It was dark when the one-horse buggy stopped outside the sheriff's office. The man who stepped down wearily to the hard-packed road exhaled a long, tired sigh which disturbed the hairs of his thick, grey moustache. He was a stoop shouldered man, a condition which, effectively, lessened his height by several inches. Even so, the natural broadness of his physique coupled with a tendency to overweight gave him an appearance which was both imposing and distinctive. He stepped on to the boardwalk, looked up and down the street, then opened the jailhouse door and went inside.

Sheriff Cotton stopped scanning the seven rows of cards on his desk, careless of finding a place to lay the five of clubs he'd just turned over. 'Doc,' he said in greeting, because at that hour of the day it wasn't unusual for Tom Priest-pole, the only doctor in Bridger Butte, to visit the lawman in his office, 'there's coffee on the stove. Help yourself.'

Doc Priestpole filled a tin cup and walked over to the cells before speaking. 'This ain't a social visit, Bob. I'm told your prisoner here is in need of my services.'

Bob Cotton's indifference to Ethan Brodie's injuries was all too evident in the tone of his answer. 'I've got a prisoner, true enough, but I'm not sure he has any ailment that needs treatment from you. A few cuts and bruises. They'll heal themselves.'

'Man was strung between two trees and struck with a rifle butt. Could have broken ribs. Best let me in to take a look at him.'

The doc's response captured the sheriff's attention. 'Who told you that?'

'John Hartley.'

'Hartley!' Bob Cotton got to his feet. 'When did you see him?'

'Just come from his place.'

111

'Is his wife back home?'

'No. Let me in to check out this prisoner and I'll tell you what I know.'

Ethan had approached the front of the cell to listen to the conversation between the sheriff and the doctor but Bob Cotton waved him back to sit on his bunk while the door was opened. 'Don't try to make a break for it,' he warned Ethan. 'You wouldn't be the first unarmed prisoner I'd put a bullet into for trying to escape.'

Ethan said nothing, more interested in the cheerful wink the doc gave him, a wink that may have meant that the sheriff's bark was worse than his bite, but which definitely implied that he, Ethan, had nothing to worry about.

Silently, Doc Priestpole examined the injuries to Ethan's face then got him to remove his shirt so that he could check out Ellen Hartley's administrations. Satisfied that the damage to Ethan was not serious he turned his attention back to the sheriff. 'That's eighty cents the town owes me for attending a prisoner.'

He held out his hand to show that payment was now due.

Bob Cotton locked the cell door before crossing over to his desk. From the bottom drawer he withdrew a small tin box with a hinged lid. Inside, below a handful of paper receipts, lay a few coins. He picked out the required amount and dropped it into the waiting palm. 'Ellen Hartley,' he reminded the doctor. 'You got something to tell me about her? Her husband was all fired up when he hit town earlier today. Reckoned his wife had been kidnapped. Pointed the finger at my prisoner. That's why he's behind bars now.'

Doc Priestpole chuckled. 'John Hartley's the sort of man who always expects the worst. Ellen Hartley hasn't been kidnapped. I took her out to Big Timber Valley. Her sister's baby decided to find out what was going on in the world three weeks before he should have done. John just hadn't found the note Ellen left behind. He'd probably still be yelling outrage if I hadn't dropped by to tell him that Ellen is staying with her sister for a couple of days.'

The sheriff looked across to the cells where Ethan Brodie was leaning against the bars listening to the doctor's tale. 'Suppose I'll have to let him go,' he said, his mumbled words more a directive to himself than an opening gambit for a discussion with his friend.

Nonetheless, Doc Priestpole spoke again, his words making it evident that releasing Ethan Brodie was the only thing the sheriff could do. 'When he calmed down,' he said, 'John Hartley told me about your prisoner. Asked me to tell you that everything he said was true. His wife had found him bound and beaten and his horse had been stolen. He'd borrowed a horse and rifle and gone off to recover them.' He paused, jiggled the coins in his hand for a moment before tucking them into the small right-hand pocket of his waist-coat. 'Since horse and gun have been returned to the ranch,' he added, 'it seems reasonable to assume he's got his own back like he's claimed.'

The cell keys hung on a hook on the side of the desk. Bob Cotton collected them and strolled over to the cells. This confirmation that Ethan Brodie hadn't been involved in the hold-up of the stagecoach or the subsequent killing of Siggi Larrsen and Joe Dumbril wasn't a surprise to him. Earlier, he and Ben Blackett had ridden out to the crossing point of the Dearborn River and had come across the dead Diamond-D horse. They'd pushed on across the river hoping to come across three men afoot but in that they had been unsuccessful. They had found neither men nor riderless horses at the spot described to them by Ethan Brodie. Waning sunlight had prevented a prolonged search of the area and they had been forced to return to town.

'OK,' said Sheriff Cotton to his prisoner, 'you're free to go.' He unlocked the door and swung it wide. Ethan Brodie collected his hat from his bunk then followed the lawman back to his desk. 'If I need to find you will you be at your sister's house?' Bob Cotton asked.

'You won't have any trouble finding me, sheriff. Someone stole my Colt and I want it back. You know the people who were jostling me when I got to town so I suggest you start with them.' The authority in Ethan's voice startled the sheriff. 'And,' Ethan continued, 'in the morning I'll ride out with you to the Diamond-D. I've got no interest in pressing charges against the men who attacked me, nor for stealing my horse now that I have it back, but if they are the same men that robbed the stage and killed the guard you'll need me to identify them.'

Sheriff Cotton and Doc Priestpole exchanged glances. 'Ride out to the Diamond-D,' exclaimed Bob Cotton. 'I've got no authority out there. I'm sheriff here in Bridger Butte and, by consent of the people up there, I keep the peace in Enterprise, too.'

'Two men have been killed, sheriff. I think finding their killers gives you the authority to look where you will. Surely Luther Drummond won't protect road agents and murderers.'

Ethan's words elicited no response from the sheriff. Doc Priestpole looked from one man to the other noting the rigid determination in the younger man's face and the reluctance in the other. 'Reckon this fellow has a point, Bob. If you free him because he's innocent you've got to find those that are guilty. You've got an angry town on your hands. Both Joe Dumbril and Siggi Larrsen were liked and respected. You can't brush their killings under the carpet.'

'I know that,' growled Bob Cotton. 'No one suggested that they would be. I just need to look around Gunner Pass first of all. There may be clear signs there that will lead to the robbers.'

'You've already got clear signs, sheriff,' said Ethan. 'You've got my horse at the scene. You've got a link with riders from the Diamond-D, one of whom is known to be badly injured and one of whom has a dead horse. Check with the ranch foreman. He'll know who rode that horse.'

'And if he doesn't,' butted in Doc Priestpole, 'just ask Ellen Hartley who she saw riding Mr Brodie's horse after it was stolen.'

Bob Cotton threw a worried look at his friend. 'She told you who it was?'

The doctor shook his head. 'No. I haven't spoken with her on the subject, but if I understand her husband aright she's able to name the fellow and unless I miss my guess the name she'll give will present you with a wagonload of trouble.'

A frown creased the sheriff's brow and his eyes lost their brightness, telltale signs which, to the watchful Ethan Brodie, indicated that the doctor's prophesy was a reflection of Bob Cotton's own worry and its manifestation a long expected event that he'd hoped to avoid. Eventually, the lawman spoke, directing his question to Doc Priestpole. 'Did you say that Mrs Hartley intends to stay out at Big Timbers for a few days?'

'I did.'

'Perhaps I can settle this business without her involvement. I'll ride out to the Diamond-D tomorrow. Speak to the wrangler about missing horses and the foreman about injured ranch-hands.'

'If Luther Drummond will allow it,' murmured Doc Priestpole.

'No reason why he shouldn't,' Bob Cotton responded but there was an absence of conviction in his tone. Doc Priestpole shrugged his shoulders, a gesture meant to signify the end of his interest in the conversation. He pulled up another chair to the desk and placed it opposite the one that, earlier, had been occupied by the sheriff. He gathered in the cards, shuffled them and, in accordance with their nightly ritual, waited for Bob Cotton to join him.

Before leaving the two friends to their game, Ethan Brodie extracted a promise from Sheriff Cotton that, in the morning, they would ride out to the Diamond-D together. With that agreement secured, Ethan made his way to his sister's home.

Ethan had never before met his sister's husband but it took little more than a firm handshake to establish a rapport between them. Jim Claymore set an immediate humorous tone to the conversation by announcing that he was always happy to offer discounted legal charges to imprisoned family members. He was three or four inches short of Ethan's height and his hair was fine and fair above a long, oval face. His expression was friendly and his eyes clear, hinting at a man who observed and judged events with an open and inquiring mind. Over dinner, both husband and wife expressed satisfaction with the news that Ellen Hartley was no longer missing, although Irene added that

John Hartley's half-cocked accusation was typical of the man. 'I don't know that I've ever spoken more than half a dozen words to him,' she told her brother, 'but I understand he's hard working and devoted to Ellen. But he's suspicious of everyone. Seldom comes to town unless he wants something from the stores that is too heavy for Ellen to collect and never attends social events, which must be hard on Ellen. Of course they've lived here longer than Jim and I; their land was passed on to them by Ellen's folks. I sometimes wonder if it's that that troubles John Hartley. You know, if he thinks people suspect he married Ellen just to get his hands on the ranch.'

Ethan shook his head and smiled. 'It sure is good land. Might be tempted to marry someone myself if she had range land like that to lure me.'

Although aware that her brother was teasing her, Irene was eager to know if there was any special girl in his life. Despite the fact they had corresponded during the six years that had elapsed since they'd last met, his letters were infrequent and rarely containing more information than that he was in good health and satisfied with his life in San Francisco. Occasionally, he would mention visits to towns in California, Kansas or New Mexico in the pursuance of his employment, but he never wrote about the people he knew, neither male nor female, which meant that most of his life was a mystery to her. What she did know was that he was employed as a Pinkerton detective and it was with the hope of using that expertise that Irene had invited him to Montana. But, anxious as she was to discuss with her brother the situation in Bridger Butte, her pleasure at seeing him settled in a comfortable chair in her own home drove troublesome matters to the back of her mind. Instead, the threesome sat around getting acquainted over strong coffee and a bottle of French brandy which Jim Claymore had ordered especially for his brother-in-law's visit.

In fact it was Ethan who eventually broached the subject that Irene had hinted at in her last letter. 'Tell me about the trouble here in Bridger Butte, and how you think I can help.'

'Well the trouble isn't here in town,' Irene replied. 'If it were then perhaps Sheriff Cotton would do something about it. As it is, he doesn't have any jurisdiction beyond the limits of this town and Enterprise.' She paused and regarded her husband who was watching her over the rim of his coffee cup. 'In truth,' she added, 'there may not be anything illegal happening at all and if there is it may be nothing that you or anyone else can do anything about.'

Ethan shuffled in his seat. He'd just completed a long journey because he thought his sister needed urgent help. Now it seemed as though she was telling him that his effort had been unnecessary. He put his own cup of coffee on a nearby table and fixed her with a look he'd often used when trying to get information out of people. 'Tell me about your suspicions,' he told her, 'then let me be the judge of what I can do about it.'

'OK,' said Irene, 'but we need to wait until Claire arrives. I've insisted that she stays here until after her father's funeral. We have sufficient rooms. And,' she added, as though it was an afterthought, 'I don't want her to be alone tonight.' Ethan noted the look that passed between his sister and her husband and figured that it carried a message that her concern for the girl was greater than a show of compassion for the death of her father.

Almost before Irene's words had died in the room there was a light tap at the door and her husband stepped across the room to open it. Claire Dumbril wore a plain, cavalry-blue dress which had a small white collar and three small white buttons on the bodice as decoration. Around her shoulders was a brown, knitted shawl, the ends of which she gripped tightly in her left hand. In her right she held a leather bag which Jim Claymore took from her and put down at the foot of the far staircase. For a moment she stood motionless just inside the room. With the change of attire from when he'd seen her at the jailhouse, Ethan also saw a change of expression on her face. Gone was the overt glare of anger and the tears of outrage induced by the sudden news of her father's death. Now she appeared as calm and well-groomed as a seamstress at a Sunday Meeting. Her long, fair hair was held back from her face by a length of maroon ribbon and she held herself in a posture that declared an attitude of determination. Her shoulders were back and her chin was up and, in turn, she looked unwaveringly into the eyes of everyone in the room. Irene took her arm and brought her forward to meet her brother, this introduction being more formal than the one that had taken place earlier in Bob Cotton's office. Claire didn't smile; she had adopted an expression of stoic determination to hide the turmoil within and, having adopted it, had, presently, lost the ability to change it.

In the course of his career as a detective, Ethan had seen many people who had had to come to terms with sudden tragedy, so he was not disconcerted by Claire Dumbril's unflinching gaze. Indeed, he admired the strength of purpose it showed but, more than that, he was surprised to find that he was studying and appreciating the startling blue of the eyes that looked at him. Momentarily, he felt uneasy. This was a girl in mourning.

It was Claire, however, who spoke first. 'You've come to help us, Mr Brodie.' Her words were neither a question nor a statement, yet they needed a response because, unlike Irene's written messages, they were delivered with a tang of despair and a hint of hope.

'The name is Ethan,' he said, 'and

until I hear the full story I don't know what I can do.'

Over the next hour the story was related to Ethan. Jim Claymore, in his lawyer manner, laid out the bare facts which Irene embellished with details. A bad winter had been the harbinger of recent events. Snow came early and unexpectedly. Temperatures dropped to way below zero making it difficult for the hands to get to the cattle and much of the stock was left to fend for itself on the open range. No outfit escaped without heavy losses. Come spring, there were carcasses all along the valley of the Dearborn. Herds were depleted and ranches, large and small, faced financial hardship. But a winter loss wasn't the only thing the ranchers shared. They all had a desire to succeed and though more than one of the small ranchers had to make new arrangements with the bank to prevent foreclosure on their mortgage, no one spoke of quitting their land. The task of rebuilding their herd began.

It was a man called Adams who first moved out. The Dearborn was the boundary line between his spread and the Diamond-D ranch. Luther Drummond let it be known that he intended to build a larger herd than he'd had the previous year and, come another winter, with the lower pastures of the Adams' spread close to his own home range, he'd be able to bring his cattle down from the high country early and avoid another heavy loss. At first, it surprised people that Adams sold his land but they reasoned that without a family he was perhaps wise to sell up and escape the multitude of worries a cattleman faces every time he gets out of bed.

'Of course,' said Irene, 'Chet Adams leaving his ranch wasn't the only thing that surprised people hereabouts. Most of the talk was centred on Luther Drummond's ability to buy it. He hadn't come through the winter unscathed, in fact he'd probably lost more head of cattle than any of the ranchers, so his proclamation to build a larger herd coupled with his ability to buy out Chet Adams set people to wondering how rich he was. Then he made a bid for Johnny Harper's land and we all began wondering just how much territory the Drummonds need.' Irene threw a quick glance in Claire's direction and Ethan followed his sister's look. Claire sat upright in a high winged chair, her hands in her lap, her head slightly bowed. Sensing the looks that had been cast her way she raised her head. The determination that Ethan had sensed earlier was again apparent as her blue eyes met his own in unwavering fashion. 'Johnny and Claire were engaged,' explained Irene. 'He had no wish to sell his land. He was improving the old house to take Claire there as his wife.'

Claire took up the story with dramatic words delivered in a tone of ice. 'They killed him,' she said.

Jim Claymore, lending his professional knowledge to the conversation, interrupted. 'We have no proof of that. For all we know Johnny is still alive.' Any argument he may have felt duty bound to expound on that theory was stopped by a critical look from his wife.

Claire spoke again. 'Johnny refused to sell. He went to the bank and had his mortgage extended so that he could buy more stock. Rustlers ran off those new, young, steers within a week of Johnny bringing them to Montana. While he was riding the range looking for a trace of his stolen stock, his ranch house was burned to the ground and a few days later his top hand was found dead. Sheriff Cotton called it an accidental death but Johnny suspected that Luther Drummond had had some part to play in it.' She paused, contemplating the events she had related. 'It meant,' she began again, 'that Johnny couldn't hold on to his land. The bank wouldn't extend any more credit and were preparing to confiscate the ranch. As much as Pa and I wanted to help him, and others, too, it wasn't possible. Every man had his own struggle. So, when Luther Drummond stepped in with a renewed and much reduced offer, Johnny had no choice but to accept it. The money he got was barely enough to pay off his creditors. Pa wanted him to work on our ranch. It would have become ours eventually, but Johnny was too proud. Didn't want people to say he'd married me for the land. Had to have his own place.' She paused a moment, gathering her thoughts. 'He has an uncle in Santa Fe,' she continued, 'he manages the railroad freight yards and was able to guarantee Johnny a job there.' Claire paused again, her face turning to Irene who gave her a nod of encouragement to continue with her story.

'Johnny never got to Santa Fe,' she said. 'His uncle and I have exchanged messages. There is just no trace of him.'

Ethan didn't speak. Just because Johnny Harper hadn't reached Santa Fe didn't mean he was dead. Once on the trail, some chance encounter could have caused a change of plan. He waited for Claire to continue.

'It's not the fact that he didn't arrive at Santa Fe that troubles me,' she began. 'At least, it's not that alone. It's Dagg Drummond.'

'He pesters Claire,' said Irene. 'Always has. Leering and making unwelcome comments even when Johnny was with her. Set out to belittle Johnny. That's why I don't want her on her own tonight.'

Claire spoke. 'After Johnny set off for Santa Fe Dagg started dropping by our ranch. I made it clear I didn't want him there and Pa chased him off with his shotgun a couple of times. Dagg laughed at us. Said that I'd have a long wait if I expected Johnny to send for me. Said it like he knew Johnny hadn't gone to Santa Fe, as though he knew where he was. Pa was real angry. Threatened to go and see Luther Drummond and tell him to keep his son away from our spread. But then things started happening to us the way they'd happened to Johnny. Mysterious fires in the barns and stables. Some of our steers were stampeded over a bluff and those that weren't killed outright we had to slaughter. More carcasses in the meadow, more lost investment. Then rumours started around town that Pa couldn't pay his workers and we found it difficult to get riders to handle the steers. Finally, a waterhole was poisoned. We lost a hundred head and, like Johnny, with no prospect of profit for a second year, the bank foreclosed on us.'

'Tell Ethan what that skunk did,' said Irene.

Claire Dumbril looked down at her hands which were still clasped together in her lap. 'He said that when the bank took possession of our land the Diamond-D would buy it at a bargain price. But he said there was a way that Pa could keep his ranch. The price was me. If I married him the land would only be absorbed into the Drummond Empire after Pa died. He sneered at me when I refused. Told me I was wasting my time waiting for Johnny to come for me. Said he was never coming back. There was such a certainty in his words that I knew Johnny was dead.' She looked across at Ethan's brother-in-law. 'I know there's no proof to take to the sheriff or a court,' she told him, 'but I still know that Dagg Drummond killed Johnny.' She turned her attention back to Ethan Brodie. 'Pa knew it too. He said he'd rather lose his ranch than see me married to Dagg Drummond. So we moved into town. I help Irene with the school and Pa took a job with the stagecoach company. But now he's dead too.

9

Saturday morning was usually a time of unhurried companionship in the Claymore household. There was no school that day to demand Irene's attention and experience had taught Jim that it was a day when the citizens around Bridger Butte had little need of a lawyer. As a result, he only opened his office after noon which, in the main, was to give him the opportunity to keep up to date with paperwork and matters of administration. This Saturday morning, however, with two guests in the house, there was a different, more cautious atmosphere.

Irene, fussing in a manner peculiar to women entertaining in their own home, arranged table settings for breakfast then, rejecting Claire Dumbril's offer of assistance, retired to the cooking area to prepare food and coffee. She hummed the tune of a popular ballad while she worked.

Jim Claymore was less hearty this morning than he'd been the previous night, affected, no doubt, by the young, mourning girl who sat opposite. Claire, dressed this morning in trousers and heavy wool shirt, sat in the parlour with Jim and Ethan. She was quiet, contemplating the events of the day ahead that had never been envisaged. They would bury her father at sundown. Before then she needed to talk to the undertaker and Cy Dando to make sure there would be no hitches. Although not ordained by any church, Cy Dando did whatever preaching was necessary in these parts. The town didn't have a regular church and in the last fifteen years folks could only remember two visits from a circuit preacher. Seven and a half years seemed too long a wait for most people who needed to be christened, married or buried so Cy said words and led those congregated in the singing of a hymn. They may not

have been the words proscribed th
true authorities but the people   b
Bridger Butte accepted them w   w
same solemnity they'd have affo   d
skirted priest. Jim offered to m   c
visits on Claire's behalf, bu   C
refused. Performing the tasks   n
would get her out of the   o
Although grateful for the hospita   d
the Claymores, she suspected th   r
desire for revenge for the unnec
killing of her father was causing   s
some embarrassment. James Clay   p
was, after all, a lawyer who though   s
punishment should be handed out   p
court. Ethan Brodie had promise
do what he could but she figured
had a role to play herself. If displ
her grief aroused some action from
sheriff and the townsfolk then she
no reason to hide it.

Ethan Brodie's thoughts were
tred on Bob Cotton. Last night,
sheriff had readily agreed with Etha
request to accompany him to
Diamond-D. In the light of a new d

e alacrity with which that pact had
een adopted could only be viewed
ith suspicion. Lawmen, Ethan knew,
dn't like civilians around when
onducting official business, so Bob
otton's eagerness could have been
othing more than a ruse to get him
ut of the office so that he and the
octor could concentrate on their
ightly card game.

On the plus side, however, the
tagecoach hold-up had angered many
eople in the town and perhaps the
heriff was truly anxious to get the
eople responsible as soon as possible.

Ethan's concern that the sheriff
would proceed without him was soon
aid to rest. Irene had barely transferred
the ham and eggs from skillet to plate
before a youthful, high pitched voice,
yelled his name from the street. Ethan
opened the door and was confronted by
a gangly lad about twelve years old. He
wore grubby jeans and a red plaid shirt
and was bare-headed. His left hand was
thrust deep into his trouser pocket.

Behind the lad, Ethan could see his horse hitched to a rail. The lad indicated the horse with a head motion. 'Sheriff told me to saddle him and give you a message.' Ethan waited for the message. 'Sheriff says he'll be riding past here in five minutes. You need to be ready if you're going with him.'

Ethan cast an eye over the horse which had carried him staunchly over the past few days. It deserved a rest and the slight droop of its head indicated that it needed one. He had planned to hire a horse from the livery stable for the day but he couldn't switch mounts in five minutes. 'Tell the sheriff I'll be waiting for him,' he told the lad and flipped him a dime before heading back indoors.

★ ★ ★

The day was warm and there was a well worn trail to the Diamond-D. Once clear of the town Bob Cotton set the pace, urging his mount into a brisk canter. Ethan Brodie matched him pace for pace and they rode without conversation for half an hour. Once again, Ethan was impressed by the country through which they passed. The quality of the grazing land was finer than anything that Texas or New Mexico had to offer. The meadows were greener and more lush prompting the thought that, despite the summer heat he'd encountered, there must be water a-plenty throughout the year.

They halted on a slight rise overlooking a clear, fast-moving stream. Pointing first in the direction of the rivulet's flow, Bob Cotton informed Ethan that the water merged into the Dearborn at a point two miles east. Then he pointed straight ahead, across the stream. 'Luther Drummond's ranch house lies beyond that fold of hills. We'll be there in ten minutes. I'll do the talking. If you recognize any of the men who attacked you just keep it to yourself until I ask you to point them out. Is that clear?'

Ethan said that it was. Before they moved on, the sheriff reached into his saddle-bag and brought out the Colt that Ethan had lost when he'd been dragged from his horse. He knew Bob Cotton wouldn't tell him who had taken it so he simply checked that the chambers were full and slid it into its holster. They walked the horses down to the stream, across it and up through a pass between two low hills which led into a wide open meadow. Bob Cotton spurred his horse into a canter again and for several minutes they rode without anything by way of sight, sound or smell to suggest that people lived or worked anywhere between here and the Canadian border. But then they came up from a grassy depression and before them was a three-pole fence which stretched east and west across their path. Carrying on the air was the lowing of cattle. Far to their left was a herd consisting of between two and three hundred head and Ethan fancied he could distinguish three riders working among them though they were too far away to identify.

Bob Cotton led the way west along the fence until they came to a gateway set between poles almost fifteen feet high. At the highest point a board swung on ropes on which was painted in black a diamond shape with a D inside and below the name Luther Drummond. They stopped at the gate. Beyond, Ethan could see a low ranch house building which seemed to straggle over a large area, as though the original building had been extended in a haphazard manner although never upwards. He could see other buildings clustered around a yard, barns, bunkhouse, storage sheds and stables, and further to the left, almost behind the last building, there was a massive corral containing at least fifty horses. Intermingled with the high whinny of two or three of those beasts were the shouts of the men cajoling the dumb animals, a sound which carried across the yard to where Bob Cotton and Ethan Brodie had paused. Then another shout went up, this one more clear, more threatening and directed at the new arrivals.

In a swirl of dust a rider galloped swiftly towards the gate yelling questions and instructions as he approached. 'Who are you? What do you want here. Keep away from that gate.' When he dragged his horse to a halt he peered through the dust at the people he berated. 'Bob Cotton?' he queried, 'is that you?'

'Sure is,' replied the sheriff. 'Open the gate. I need to speak to Luther.'

The man's attention was focused on Ethan, and more especially on Ethan's horse. 'This the man you arrested for the hold-up?' Sheriff Cotton told him it was. 'Hear he's been making accusations against Diamond-D riders. Boss won't be pleased you've brought him here.'

'Still need to talk to him,' said Bob Cotton. 'Open the gate, Gus.'

The three riders sat looking at each other and, for a moment, it seemed that Gus wouldn't open the gate, then, slowly, with a sigh of resignation, he reached forward and undid the fastening. Ethan and Bob Cotton passed through and headed toward the ranch house. 'That's Gus Hardin,' Bob informed Ethan, indicating the man riding behind them. 'He's foreman here at the Diamond-D.' Ethan glanced back at the brawny man with the grey, grizzly beard but the foreman wore a look of disdain, as though suggesting that their paths would never cross again after this day.

Gus Hardin wasn't the only man whose attention was captured by the distinctive horse under Ethan Brodie. As the trio headed towards the ranch house a couple of ranch-hands outside the bunk house broke off their conversation to watch them pass by and a wrangler, working with a raw mustang near the corral, drew the attention of some others to the new arrivals. By the time the group had reached the ranch house a handful of men had gathered round expectantly.

Gus Hardin called to the house from the saddle. 'Mr Drummond.'

Several moments passed before the door opened. Luther Drummond stepped on to the porch and studied the two mounted men ranged alongside his foreman. He was a short man, no more than five feet four inches high, but he was broad with a deep chest and long arms. He had little neck, his big head with its wide face seeming to sprout directly from his shoulders. His mouth was wide with thin lips and his nose was broad but straight. His eyes were so narrow that it was impossible to discern any colour. Overall it was the face of a cautious man, a man who kept his own counsel and controlled others by ensuring strict adherence to his rules. His features were not softened by any semblance of pleasure.

'Bob Cotton,' he said, his lips barely moving, his words passing through the air like a low growl. 'You've got no business on Diamond-D land.'

'Yesterday's stage was robbed, Luther. Two men killed.'

'I heard. None of my business and none of yours. Federal marshal investigates highway robberies, not small town sheriffs.'

'The men killed were from Bridger Butte. I reckon that makes it my business.'

Luther Drummond dismissed Bob Cotton's words with a grunt then, extending his left arm, pointed at Ethan Brodie. 'This the fellow who's accusing Diamond-D riders?'

Ethan sat still in the saddle, his hands resting lightly on the saddle horn. Bob Cotton spoke. 'This is Ethan Brodie. There was an incident yesterday at the river crossing south of town. Brodie here took a beating and his horse was stolen. Indications are that some of your men were involved.'

'Wrong,' snapped Luther Drummond. 'All my men are accounted for.'

'That's right,' said Gus Hardin. 'We had everyone working yesterday but no one had reason to be on the new range. We've got no cattle there at present. Won't be for a few weeks, until we bring them down from the high country before the weather changes.'

Bob Cotton looked around at the curious ranch-hands. 'One of the men,' he told them, 'took some blows to the head from Siggi Larssen. Won't be able to hide his injuries. Way I understand it he's in need of a doctor.' When no one responded he rubbed his jaw then directed a question at the ranch foreman. 'Lost any horses recently, Gus?'

Gus Hardin threw a cautious look at his boss but Luther Drummond kept his unblinking gaze on the sheriff. 'You mean stolen?'

'Stolen. Thrown a rider and run-off. Not accounted for,' clarified Bob Cotton.

'No.'

'There's a dead horse near the

crossing point. Got your brand on it. Perhaps you should ride down and look at it. Tell me who it belongs to.'

'You're forgetting yourself, sheriff,' growled Luther Drummond. 'You don't give orders around here, I do. And I'm telling you to get off my land. You've got no authority here.'

'Luther,' began Bob Cotton, but he got no further.

'When you come uninvited on to my land and make unfounded charges against my men on the word of some saddle tramp then you call me Mr Drummond.'

Bob Cotton held the other's angry gaze. 'Very well, Mr Drummond, but this man's story checks out. He was attacked without cause, his horse stolen and whoever stole it held up the stagecoach. Perhaps he can't identify the men who did it but I suspect that Ellen Hartley can. She saw them riding off in the direction of Gunner Pass. Now there are two good men to bury. Believe me, Mr Drummond, with or without your help the law will hunt out those responsible.'

Bob Cotton would have turned his horse at that point and made his way back to the gateway, but Ethan Brodie leaned forward and spoke for the first time. 'Makes you think, doesn't it, Mr Drummond.' Luther Drummond didn't respond. 'You've recently purchased the land of both dead men.'

'What's that supposed to mean?'

'It's interesting, that's all. You purchase the ranches of Siggi Larrsen, Joe Dumbril and Johnny Harper and now two of them are dead and one missing.'

Luther Drummond couldn't hide his surprise at Ethan's words. 'Missing?'

'Yes. Johnny Harper. Never did get to his uncle's home at Santa Fe but I'm sure you know that already.' Drummond struggled to keep his features the inscrutable mask they always were. 'Your son knows. Which reminds me, where is he? I have a message for him.'

'My son. He's rounding up stock in the north pastures. What message?'

'It's from Miss Dumbril. She doesn't want him bothering her anymore. If he thinks she'll accept his advances now that her father is dead he couldn't be more wrong. And she has a new protector. Me. So tell him to stay on the ranch, Mr Drummond, or he'll find himself in more trouble than he can handle.'

Anger flared in Luther Drummond's tight little eyes. His cheeks darkened with fury. 'How dare you come making threats to my family on my land. Get off this ranch before I have you thrown off.'

'Just delivering a message, Mr Drummond. If you don't want to pass it on I might ride up north and tell him myself.'

'You get off my land and stay off. If you're caught trespassing I'll have you shot.'

Ethan touched his hat, grinned and sarcastically said, 'Your hospitality has been overwhelming.' Then he turned his horse and galloped back to the gateway with Bob Cotton at his heels.

If working for the Pinkerton Detective Agency had taught Ethan Brodie anything it was that to stir up activity on a case it was sometimes necessary to put yourself out on a limb. Hence his behaviour at the Diamond-D. It was apparent to him that Luther Drummond considered himself the custodian of the law in matters concerning the Diamond-D and in matters that didn't, he had no interest. No matter what argument Bob Cotton put to him about the hold-up he was not going to get any assistance from the rancher. However, Luther Drummond's surprise when Ethan had spoken of Johnny Harper's disappearance had seemed genuine enough although Ethan knew for certain that his son was aware of it. Claire Dumbril had spoken the night before of Dagg Drummond's sneering attitude to the absence of her fiancé. So he had thrown down the gauntlet to Luther's son, believing, as was usual with men

151

who tried to build an empire, that they sought to found a dynasty, that their name should carry the same authority in the future that they had established in the beginning. Luther would want Dagg to rule the Diamond-D after he'd gone and any threat to that would have to be averted.

Ethan had encountered several men of ambition and authority, the smart ones only resorted to violence when they knew it couldn't be traced to them. Luther Drummond, Ethan surmised, despite his blunt appearance and insular attitude, was not a stupid man. He would want to know all the details before taking on a challenge to his authority. Ethan guessed that the first thing Drummond would do would be to send Gus Hardin to look at the dead horse and apprise him of its owner. Also, Ethan thought, he would send for his son to determine the truth about Johnny Harper. After that he would decide what to do about Ethan.

Sheriff Cotton had no cause for

hesitation. Before they were half a dozen strides beyond the Diamond-D gateway he lashed out at Ethan with a startling string of oaths and curses, belaying him for breaking his word and invoking Luther Drummond's ire. 'A lot of businesses in Bridger Butte survive on the trade the Diamond-D throws their way.'

'He's angry with me, not the people of Bridger Butte.'

'And me,' declared Bob Cotton. 'He won't forget that I took you there.'

'You were doing your duty, Sheriff. If he'd offered you the assistance you required I wouldn't have had to goad him.'

'You did that on purpose?'

'Sure. Bet a dollar he sends someone to the south crossing to check out that dead horse. Want to ride over there with me and see who turns up?' Bob Cotton shook his head. Ethan exerted a little pressure. 'If Drummond isn't around, that badge you're wearing might be sufficient to extract some answers.'

'I've got a town to run,' he told Ethan, 'besides, he already knew who you were. Seems to me that if he'd already heard your claim about being beaten by Diamond-D riders he'd know, too, about the dead horse. Probably sent someone to look at it yesterday.'

Ethan shook his head. 'If Drummond and his foreman had known they'd have prepared a story in advance of your visit, Sheriff. No, the fact that there is evidence against the Diamond-D came as a surprise and if I'm any judge of people I'd say that Luther Drummond is the kind of man who needs to know all there is to know before he acts.'

Bob Cotton looked at Ethan Brodie with a wary expression. Eventually, he spoke. 'Let me give you a word of advice, Brodie,' he said. 'You're a stranger in these parts and blood and death has come to the valley with you. Most people in town don't take to strangers and even those that do aren't sure how much of yesterday's trouble is down to you. Be careful. Don't go causing trouble with the Diamond-D because that's a fight you can't win.' Those were the sheriff's parting words. He spurred his horse forward in the direction of Bridger Butte and Ethan sat for a while and watched him go. Then he touched his spurs to his horse's flanks and headed him east, in the direction that the stream flowed to its junction with the Dearborn.

10

Among the cowhands gathered to hear the exchange between their boss and the sheriff was a young, pale faced youth with a heavy, drooping moustache. With his thumbs hooked into his gunbelt he leant against the hitching rail outside the ranch house and watched the visitors ride away. No emotion showed on his face but in his mind the desire for revenge overtook all other thoughts. If, yesterday, in the street melee when the mob had been fixed on a lynching, there had been any doubt that the rider of the distinctive horse was not the Pinkerton agent responsible for the killing of his brother Nate, then today, with time for a close study of the man, all doubt was removed. It was essential to pass on that information to his eldest brother, Fitz.

Fitz Collier had been away from the ranch for three days, part of a crew riding herd on the east range across the Dearborn. Sometime today he would return. The pale faced cowboy watched as the sheriff and Ethan Brodie paused beyond the compound fence line then, after an exchange of words, saw them put spurs to their mounts. At the same time his attention was caught by the approach of three riders from the east. A tight grin stretched his lips when he recognized the high-arm riding style of one of the men. It was his brother.

'Fitz,' he called as soon as the riders were within hailing distance. 'Over here. Got something to tell you.'

Fitz Collier pulled his horse alongside his brother. There was a similarity in the colour of their eyes, their hair and in the predominance of their nose, but the shape of their faces differed. Unlike his brother, Fitz was clean shaven and swarthy. He looked down at his brother but before any conversation began, a call from the ranch house steps

157

demanded his immediate attention. 'Speak to you later, Cal,' he said then rode to where Luther Drummond stood with Gus Hardin. 'You want me, boss?'

'Go with Gus to the south crossing,' Luther commanded. 'If it's needed give him some protection.'

'You expecting trouble, Mr Drummond?'

'Could be. There's a stranger trying to stir things up. If he shows up make sure he gets the message that he's not welcome around here. Don't kill him. Seems the sheriff puts some store by the story he's telling. Rough him up enough to chase him out of the territory.'

Fitz nodded and waited for Gus to mount up. Together they rode towards the boundary gate. Cal tried once more to speak to his brother. 'Later,' called Fitz as the horses gathered speed and kicked up dust.

* * *

The dead horse was beginning to smell. Flies swarmed around the bullet hole in its head like a veil disturbed by the breeze. Ethan tethered his horse in good pasture out of sight of the trail and away from the spot where the carcass lay. He climbed on to the sturdy bough of a nearby oak where he settled into an eyrie-like network of branches and leaves. This location provided him with a modicum of comfort and a great deal of concealment. It also gave him a commanding view of the trail from Bridger Butte down to the river and also the riverbank trail that he had followed from the Diamond-D. The dead horse was no more than twenty yards away, close enough for Ethan to identify the brand of the Diamond D on its rump and observe anyone who came to investigate.

A mere ten minutes had passed when Gus Hardin came into sight, walking his horse in cautious fashion as though he wasn't simply following the course of the river but also tracking the man ahead and wary of ambush. He was watchful, his head turning first one way then another, checking the bushes and boulders for signs of a trap. He carried an uncovered rifle across his lap, a finger of his right hand inside the trigger guard. His left hand held the reins of his mount which moved in response to the pressure of knees and boots. Silently, when he saw the dead cayuse in the clearing, he drew his horse to a halt, raised the rifle so that the butt rested on his right thigh and peered around. He sat in that manner for a full minute, until he was satisfied that it was safe to dismount. Still gripping the rifle, he dropped the reins in front of his animal and walked carefully forward.

Ethan Brodie had expected Luther Drummond to send someone to check out the dead animal but he hadn't expected the man to come hunting for him. He watched as Hardin walked to within six feet of the dead beast, saw his lips move in what seemed to be a muttered oath but which was too low to carry up to his lookout position. But the look on the foreman's face couldn't be disguised.

Clearly, he recognized the mount and, just as clearly, the significance of that recognition didn't please him. Once more he cast an eye around the clearing to confirm that no one was watching, then he went back to his horse and slid the rifle into the saddle boot.

Ethan prepared to climb out of the tree suspecting that the Diamond-D man was about to climb on to his horse and report back to Luther Drummond, but he didn't. Gus Hardin drew a broad hunting knife from a sheath on his left hip and returned to the carcase. While Hardin had his back to him, Ethan swung down from the tree. 'Won't do you any good,' he said, his voice holding a hint of amusement.

Gus Hardin swung around, his right hand dropping to his holster.

'Whoa,' said Ethan. 'I'm not looking

for a fight.' He spread his arms in front of him in a placatory gesture. 'Just wanted to say that disfiguring the brand won't do you any good. I've seen it. The sheriff's seen it and others have seen it. We know it's a Diamond-D horse.'

'Stranger, what you know is a matter of no consequence around here. No one's going to take your word against the Diamond-D's. As for Bob Cotton, he'll say exactly what Luther Drummond wants him to say if he hopes to continue as sheriff of Bridger Butte. This is Diamond-D land and what Luther Drummond says is the law around here.'

'Someone spoke similar words the last time I stood in this glade,' said Ethan. 'Someone who stole my horse and nearly got me hanged for killings I didn't do.'

'Then take my advice,' said Hardin. 'Get on your horse and ride clear of Bridger Butte. Your luck may not hold much longer.'

Ethan shook his head. 'The men who

killed Joe Dumbril were Diamond-D riders. I know it and your attempt to hide the iron mark on that dead cayuse confirms it. I may not know the names but I'll recognize the men involved. I intend to see them stand trial for murder.'

Though the words were spoken in a gentle manner and the lips were parted in a hint of a smile, Gus Hardin heard the determination in the other's tone, saw it in the unflinching gaze in the other's eyes and, although the man before him seemed relaxed and easy going, he sensed a confidence that bespoke a man who saw things through to the bitter end. When Gus spoke he tried to keep the tension he felt out of the words. 'Don't make trouble.'

'Trouble's already here.'

'I'm trying to help you,' said Gus, an edge of desperation creeping into his voice.

'Then name the rider of that horse. I'll find out eventually. I'm not going away until I do.'

'Then you'll wind up in a plot next to Joe Dumbril.'

'There'll be others with me if I do.'

Unaccountably, Gus Hardin shivered. 'Are those your last words?' Ethan nodded.

With a sigh Gus turned away, began walking towards his horse. On the third stride he raised his right arm. The gesture could have been a friendly wave but, in fact, it was the signal he'd arranged earlier with Fitz Collier. Fitz had left the trail a quarter of a mile back and circled round to approach the crossing point from a different angle. For several minutes he'd loitered among the cottonwoods awaiting Gus's order.

Now he came forward, galloping into the clearing wielding a stout branch he'd gathered while he waited. At the sound of the hoof beats, Ethan turned. Instinctively, as Fitz swung the branch at his head, Ethan threw himself to his right. He rolled, unharmed, while Fitz turned his mount to renew the attack.

Again Fitz rode forward, this time at a slower pace, the horse prancing when it came alongside Ethan. When the club descended once more, Ethan stepped nearer the horse, his back pressing against its rump, too close for the attempted blow to be effective. Fitz had to re-adjust the line of his swing, effectively reducing its power. Ethan was able to grasp the arm of his adversary and for some moments they struggled. With his feet planted firmly, Ethan was almost able to pull Fitz from his saddle but Fitz, surprised by his foe's strength, used the weight of his horse to unbalance Ethan.

Eventually, Ethan released his grip on the other's arm. Swiftly, he dropped to the ground and rolled under the animal. Staying low, he grabbed Fitz's foot and heaved upwards with all his strength. With a loud yell the Diamond-D cowboy came out of the saddle and crashed on to the hard ground. Now it was Ethan's turn to use the horse. Pushing on its hindquarters he turned it into the rising Fitz who had to scuttle backwards to avoid being trampled. Ethan followed the tail around and leapt at Fitz as he tried to regain his feet. He landed a right hand punch just below Fitz's left ear which produced an oath as he sprawled in the dirt. Fitz shook his head to clear the buzzing from his ears and reacted quickly when he saw Ethan closing in on him again. Swiftly and accurately he threw a handful of dust at Ethan's face, forcing the Pinkerton man to check his advance. From the ground, Fitz launched himself at his opponent's lower legs, toppling Ethan on to his back. In an instant, the Diamond-D man was on top. He threw a left and a right at Ethan's jaw but neither connected with enough force to prove decisive. Ethan rolled, dislodged Fitz and scrambled to his knees.

By a quirk of fate the supine Fitz found the branch he had used in his initial attack close to his right hand. Gathering it, he then swung it as hard as he was able at Ethan's head. Fortunately for Ethan, leaning backwards was movement enough to take him out of range and, harmlessly, it passed by. The momentum, however, unbalanced Fitz and before he was able to steady himself to deliver another swipe, Ethan had delivered a staggering blow to his jaw followed by a vicious punch which split the skin below his left eye and left him momentarily senseless.

Fitz Collier wasn't a big man but he was strong, wiry and durable. Gus Hardin had never seen him beaten in a fist fight; no one at the Diamond-D ever had, which was why Luther Drummond had chosen him to ride with his foreman. Now, Gus was unsure what to do next. His hand strayed towards his holster and he began pulling his pistol free when he heard Ethan's words. 'Don't make me shoot you, Hardin.' Gus paused, his eyes alone continuing the sweep to align on Ethan Brodie. What he saw was a man whose Colt was already clear of its holster and pointed at the centre of his body. 'I've no reason to suspect you of any involvement with the hold-up of the stagecoach so I have no reason to kill you. But don't try to draw on me again. Next time I'll finish it.' He motioned with his gun for Gus to collect Fitz and load him on his horse. When both Diamond-D men were mounted, Ethan spoke again. 'Make your report to Luther Drummond. Tell him to bring those men into town tomorrow. They'll get a trial. If they aren't in jail by midday I'll be looking for them.'

Ethan watched the Diamond-D foreman ride out of sight, tagging the battered cowpuncher's horse along behind him. Then, seeking out his own horse, he rode back to town.

★   ★   ★

An hour later, Gus Hardin's account of the incident at the south crossing burning in his brain, Luther Drummond stomped the floor of his ranch house. The man, Brodie, had said a mouthful earlier when he'd arrived with Bob Cotton, now he was making demands and sending threats. No one had ever threatened Luther Drummond on Diamond-D land and lived. This stranger, saddle tramp, needed to be taught a lesson. Needed to know the order of things in this corner of Montana. 'Just where does he think he's going to be looking for those men? On Diamond-D land? If he so much as sits astride a horse that strays one hoof on this range then shoot him as a trespasser. Do you hear me, Gus?'

'Sure, boss.' Gus Hardin agreed, he always agreed with Luther, but this time the usual conviction in his voice was missing, a lack which didn't pass unnoticed.

'I want him dead,' snapped Luther. 'Do you hear me? Dead.'

Gus, head bowed, nodded. Momentarily, he lifted his head to look at Luther Drummond. The rancher's face was a purple mask of anger and hatred but as his eyes met his foreman's the expression changed to one of worry and confusion.

'Are you sure, Gus?' Luther's voice was weighted with concern.

The foreman understood the sudden question. 'Yes, boss,' he said. 'It was Dagg's horse. I saw him ride out on it yesterday morning.'

'What was he doing at the south crossing? He had no business there. Who was riding with him?'

'The usual three: Lou Petersen; Chad Trelawney; Charlie Tyson.'

'And they're supposed to be up on the north pastures.'

'Locating strays. Building a herd to bring down to the home range before winter.'

Luther paced the room again and rubbed at his head. It seemed to Gus that he was trying to massage his brain into action, trying to find answers to the questions he couldn't bring himself to ask aloud. When he got back to his desk Luther looked down at his sitting foreman. The question he posed was one of desperation, another attempt to side-step the real issue. 'Has something happened to Dagg? Did someone bushwhack him and steal his horse?'

'We'd have heard something. One of the others would have ridden in to let us know.'

'Perhaps they were all left afoot. Perhaps they are out there injured, trying to find their way back here.'

Gus shook his head slowly, that was a possibility too remote to consider. Besides, it was well known that the descriptions Brodie had given the sheriff were a good fit for Dagg and his partners.

Immediately, the anger which resurfaced in Luther was vented on Gus. 'You think he did it, don't you? You think Dagg robbed the stage. Why? Why would he do that? He has no need to steal money.'

For Luther's sake, Gus wanted to deny the accusation but, struggle as he would, he found it impossible to find

171

any words that would satisfy his boss and, at the same time, appease his own conscience. Typical of the pioneers who had succeeded in settling the wild land, Luther was a hard man, a man whose achievements would have been less without the discipline of the laws he'd made. He was a man with enemies but, nonetheless, respected. A man feared but esteemed. His major failure, Gus believed, was his son. Dagg had inherited his father's physical attributes and his temper, but instead of esteem and respect the fear he engendered was the result of his meanness and cruelty. Gus had always seen it; his father turned a blind eye to it.

'You think my son is a common road agent? And killer?'

Again Gus was slow to answer. Trying to evade Luther's angry gaze he tried to give a noncommittal shrug. 'It was the girl's father,' he said. 'Everyone knows Joe Dumbril told Dagg to stay away from her.'

'And you think my son killed a man

over some chit of a girl? Dagg can choose from dozens of women in these parts. What does it matter if one of them turns him down.'

Gus kept his own counsel. He'd always suspected that Claire Dumbril had been Luther's choice for his son and that forcing the old man to sell him his spread had, in some fashion, been done as an incentive for her to marry Dagg. The Dumbrils' subsequent resentment of the Drummonds had taken Luther by surprise.

Realizing his foreman had no appetite for the conversation, Luther dismissed him with a jerk of his head. 'Get my horse saddled. I'll ride up to the line shack. Dagg can answer my questions himself.'

In daylight, the north pasture was four hours away, at this time of the day, with dusk approaching, the ride might be extended by another hour. 'Why not let me go,' said Gus. 'I'll take a look at things up there and I'll start back with Dagg at first light.'

But Luther squashed any further argument with a scowl and raised hand. No sooner was his horse brought to the house than he was in the saddle. He was as fit and active as any man he employed and as much at home driving cows as he was negotiating cattle sales or balancing the ranch accounts. Nor did he need an intermediary between himself and his own son. It was his judgement that mattered and what he learned first hand would dictate how he reacted.

His final words to Gus Hardin, spoken as he rode towards the compound gate with the foreman walking at his side, were overheard by several of the ranch-hands. 'If Bob Cotton comes here tomorrow you tell him that I'm taking care of matters that involve the Diamond-D, and if that doesn't suit that fellow Brodie then the Diamond-D'll take care of him too. I don't want to hear any more accusations against my son or my riders.'

11

Two dun horses, heads lowered as though appreciating the sadness of the occasion, pulled the buckboard on which lay the plain wood coffins. Behind, wearing a long, black frock coat and a high, dusty top hat, a slim man led the procession at a steady, even pace. His years numbered beyond sixty and his face offered no contradiction to that fact. It was tanned and wrinkled and his eyes were reduced to such narrow slits from years of squinting in the sunlight that it was hard to believe that it had ever been troubled by a smile. His hair, straggling from the sides and back of his hat, was grey and unkempt. In his hands he carried a small, ragged Bible, closed, except for the index finger of his right hand which marked the page he intended to read.

Claire Dumbril, with her friend Irene

Claymore holding her left arm and Irene's husband James in close attendance to her right, came next, then behind these three came a line of mourners who constituted more than half the residents of Bridger Butte.

At the graveside, Cy Dando, the Bible carrier, raised his head to the sky as he spoke his words. His voice quavered slightly and his words hadn't the strength to carry to the those furthest from the grave but when he called for the singing of *We Shall Gather at the River* the voices of the front ranks of mourners was soon enhanced by those behind.

Ethan Brodie was among those at the rear of the congregation. He'd returned from the south crossing and made straight for the eating house which was the building next to the sheriff's office. He'd filled himself with steak and coffee and, when he'd stepped outside, the procession, led by the flat-wagon hearse, was almost upon him. Removing his hat as the coffins passed by he'd debated with himself whether or not to join the line of mourners. Such an act wasn't necessary; he hadn't known Joe Dumbril or Siggi Larrsen and, judging by the nudges and looks that passed between some of the citizens, there were still those who considered him a stranger over whom the suspicion of their murder still hung. Yet, when Claire Dumbril walked past, he knew that no one else's opinion mattered.

It was Ethan's sister, Irene, who first looked his way, inclining her head slightly to acknowledge his presence. Then Claire had turned her head towards him. With her hair tucked away inside a black bonnet her face looked longer, her cheeks less full, but her eyes were sharp and dark, without a hint of tears. Although his sister held Claire's arm he could tell that it was nothing more than a symbol of support. Claire Dumbril was strong enough in every aspect to see through the events of this day. She looked directly at Ethan, with intensity, as though imparting a message that with his help she would get vengeance for her father's death. Ethan nodded once and the cortege moved on. When he saw Bob Cotton step down from the boardwalk outside the jail, Ethan stepped into the street, too, and walked with him to the cemetery.

After the interment, Ethan strolled back to Drover Street in the company of Bob Cotton and Bullwhip Saxon. He told the sheriff of his meeting with Gus Hardin at the south crossing. 'So no matter what they do to that carcass now, sheriff, I expect you to back me when I testify that it bore the brand of the Diamond-D.'

Bob Cotton replied testily. 'I don't need you or anyone else to tell me my duty, Brodie. Despite what you think or Luther Drummond says, I stand for law and order in this town and I'll do what's necessary to achieve it.'

Ethan was silent a moment wondering if Bob Cotton was substituting law and order for a quiet life and, if that was the case, was prepared to accept Luther Drummond's word to avoid confrontation. 'Don't forget that Ellen Hartley saw that dead horse, too,' he said. 'I'd be surprised if she didn't recognize its iron mark.'

Bob Cotton gave a dissatisfied grunt and went into his office. Bullwhip, warming to the new man in town, suggested a drink in the saloon across the street. Lamps were lit in the Drover's Rope Saloon and a piano player in a black, wool coat and hard, round hat pounded on the instruments keys, accurately but inartistically. The bar tender was a slim man with a slight moustache and thinning hair. He wore a thin striped, collarless shirt. A broad, white apron covered him from the waist down. He ran off two glasses of beer from a barrel at the far end of the bar and skimmed off the foam with a wooden spatula before sliding them across the counter to Bullwhip and Ethan.

Ethan turned his back to the bar so

that he could observe the room. It was long but without a great deal of depth. There were tables scattered about, all of them round but of various diameter. Some had four chairs apportioned to them and others six. Only two were currently occupied but there was a handful of drinkers at intervals along the bar. While Bullwhip was taking his first mouthful from the glass two more customers came through the batwing doors. The front man dashed his hat against his leg, chasing the dust from it. He was a pale faced man with a neat moustache and in high humour, grinning at some remark of his partner. He glanced around the room — when his gaze fell on Ethan the grin on his face died. He paused, just inside the room and didn't move again until his partner, looking quizzically at him, passed by. They found a station at the bar to the left of Bullwhip and the second man called for beers. As they waited for their drinks their heads closed against each other as, in low voice, the first man imparted information to the other.

It was clear to Ethan that he was the subject of their huddled conversation. He recalled seeing the first cowboy twice before. He had been a vociferous member of the crowd wanting to hang Ethan when he first arrived in Bridger Butte and he'd been among the ranch-hands gathered at the Diamond-D that morning. Even so, Ethan could think of no reason why trouble should come from it. However, when Bullwhip raised again the episode when his horse was taken from him, Ethan judged it prudent to curtail that subject. He suggested taking a seat at a table where a card game was in progress.

Oblivious to Ethan's desire to end the conversation, Bullwhip spoke aloud. 'But there was no doubt about the brand on that horse,' he called as Ethan began to move away from the bar. 'Diamond-D. You saw it and the sheriff saw it. Ain't that right?'

Ethan began to move towards the

tables but a voice, high, rasping, cut through the buzz of the saloon. 'You're a liar.' Ethan turned to face the two Diamond-D riders. The first, the one who had spoken, the one Ethan had seen earlier that day, was flushed with anger and determination. The other, paler, less certain, put his glass down on the bar. 'You've been saying things against the Diamond-D,' the first man continued, 'and you're going to take them back.' He was bent slightly at the waist, his right hand poised over the butt of his pistol.

'Forget it,' said Ethan. 'I haven't any quarrel with you.'

'Wrong,' said the cowboy, charged with a sense of justification like a righteous preacher confronting a drunkard or a harlot. 'You've got a quarrel with every Diamond-D rider.'

Silence had descended on the room. The slim barman moved slowly and deliberately. Reaching below the bar he picked up the shotgun he kept there. 'Now you two fellas have a choice to make,' he said, pulling back the hammers of both barrels, 'either you chuck your guns over the counter to me or you get out of here.'

The Diamond-D cowboy regarded the shotgun with some alarm, its barrels pointed at his midriff, but it was Ethan who reacted first, his hands dropping to the buckle of his gunbelt and unfastening it. He put it on the counter and pushed it towards the bartender. 'The sheriff told me to stay out of trouble with the Diamond-D. I wouldn't want to upset him.'

The attention of those in the room now concentrated on the young Diamond-D rider who, caught between his conviction and his respect for a loaded shotgun, now seemed incapable of movement. His partner touched his arm. 'Come on, Cal. Let's get out of here.'

'This whole business is for the sheriff to sort out,' said the barman. 'You get back to the Diamond-D and leave it to him.'

The two cowboys began to edge backwards towards the door. Bullwhip, unable to resist the chance of having the last word, spoke up. 'Weren't no lie about this man's horse being stolen and there's a dead cayuse at the spot where it happened. Dead cayuse branded with the Diamond-D. Sheriff's seen it and Mrs Hartley across the river's seen it, too. Leave this fight to those involved, sonny.'

When they'd gone and someone had watched them cross the street to the saloon entrance of the Butte Hotel, the bartender offered to return Ethan's gunbelt. 'I'm going to play cards,' he said. 'I'll collect it when I leave.' And, for the next hour or so, Ethan did just that, playing poker with four other men, who, having heard the rumours that he was taking on the might of Luther Drummond, were only too pleased to share his company.

By nine o'clock that night the Drover's Rope was full. The sound of the piano could barely be heard above the conversation of the customers and Ethan, in a low stakes game found himself fifteen dollars to the good. Bullwhip was talking to Ethan, telling him that he was driving the stagecoach to Billings in the morning and wouldn't be back in Bridger Butte for five days when there was jostling of people around their table and Ethan found himself facing the cowboy called Cal and another man. This man bore a bruise under his left eye that Ethan himself had supplied earlier that day.

It was Fitz who did the talking, cajoling those at the table with dark comments that Ethan was cheating, and appealing for support from those at the nearest tables by implying that any stranger who would spread lies about the people who had made this town a thriving community wouldn't hesitate to cheat at cards. Ethan tried to let it pass without answering, noting the nervousness of his fellow players. But such a silence had developed around the table that the atmosphere was pregnant with doom.

'I don't know who you are, or what you want, but I came in here for a game of cards. I suggest you go about your business and leave me to get on with mine.'

'Need an introduction do you? Well I'll tell you who I am. I'm Fitz Collier, and this is my brother, Cal.'

'Never heard of you,' said Ethan, his tone dismissive.

'Collier,' Fitz repeated, his voice heavy with emotion and threat, 'and if I'd known who you were when we met earlier I'd have killed you on the spot.'

'You weren't up to it then,' said Ethan. 'I don't think you're up to it now.'

Bitter hatred glared in Fitz Collier's eyes. 'Think back to New Mexico, Brodie,' he said. 'Nate Collier. Nate was our brother.'

Ethan remembered Nate Collier, a cattle rustler who, along with another man, had tried to shoot it out with a posse when caught red-handed with a bunch of stolen steers. 'Your brother made his choice. Now, if you don't mind, you're disrupting our game.'

'But we do mind. You're a cheat. And not just with cards. We're calling you out, Brodie.'

The Collier boys stood side by side. Two of the players at the table stood up and moved away but Ethan rested his hands on the shoulders of the men at either side, keeping them in their seats. There wasn't yet a general awareness of the situation at Ethan's table and, because of the fullness of the room, the bartender hadn't noticed the return of Cal Collier.

'Sorry to disappoint you, boys, but I'm not wearing a gun.' Ethan kept his hands on the shoulders of his neighbours as he came to his feet proving there wasn't a gunbelt around his waist. But the hardness in Fitz Collier's eyes destroyed any possibility that this would diffuse the situation. He meant to kill Ethan and Ethan wondered if Luther Drummond had put a price on his head.

'The sheriff doesn't approve of gunfights. He wants a peaceful town,' said Ethan.

'We're doing him a favour. Keeping his town clean. So get a gun or I'll shoot you where you stand.'

'I don't think so.'

'You,' Fitz Collier spoke to the man on Ethan's right, 'give him your gun.'

Ethan pressed on the man's shoulder, a message not to move.

Fitz Collier pulled his Colt from its holster and pointed it at the man. 'Do you want to die too?'

'There's no need for that,' Ethan said. 'Here,' he selected some coins and pushed them across the table, 'you boys buy yourselves a sarsaparilla and run along home before you get into trouble.' Ethan had known from the moment he saw the Collier brothers at the table that gunplay was unavoidable. He'd chosen his words to belittle them, to disturb them, to anger them. As he spoke, he dropped another coin, seemingly by accident, so that it bounced to his left and rolled off the table. He stooped, as though to catch the coin, but went below the height of the table, pulled the pistol from the holster of the man on his left and rolled across the floor. It took only two seconds for Ethan to execute the move but they were two seconds which flummoxed the Collier boys.

By the time Fitz realized that Ethan wasn't interested in the dropped coin his target was out of sight. He fired a shot at the vacated space, the bullet smacking into the timber wall at the end of the room. Now on one knee, the pistol in Ethan's hand cracked twice. Both shots were fatal. Fitz, hit in the heart, was thrown dramatically backwards to sprawl untidily on the dirty barroom floor. Cal, too, was hit in the heart, his gun had hardly cleared leather but in his death spasm he pulled the trigger and shot himself in the foot. He never felt the pain of that self-inflicted injury.

The four gunshots brought a heavy silence to the room, as though all the occupants had breathed in at the same moment and were afraid to release it again lest it should invoke another bout of violence. Ethan stood up keeping the pistol poised as he scanned the room. 'Anyone else want to make a name for themselves?'

No one answered. The barman banged on the counter with an empty glass and the piano player struck up a lively tune. Ethan uncocked the pistol and put it on the table for his neighbour. Stuffing his pockets with the money he'd won, he addressed the other players. 'Under the circumstances, gentlemen, I think I'll call it a night.' Before he got out of the room, however, Bob Cotton, having heard the gunshots in his office across the street, swept apart the batwing doors and stood, shotgun at the ready, just across the threshold. He took in the scene at a glance, his eyes moving quickly from the bodies on the floor to Ethan Brodie,

190

his eyes agleam with accusation.

'It was self-defence, Sheriff,' said the slim bartender. 'Never seen anything like what happened over there. That man was unarmed when they picked the fight. Wouldn't believe it if I hadn't witnessed it myself.' The bartender's expression of incredulity was endorsed wholeheartedly by the other occupants of the Drover's Rope. Everyone trying to tell their own version of the event.

From the multitude of voices, Bob Cotton was able to discern one fact on which everyone agreed. Ethan Brodie had acted in self-defence, therefore, in accordance with the town law, there was no cause for arrest and trial. While such a situation would normally cause the sheriff no more bother than to note the fact in his ledger, this incident troubled him more. The dead men were riders from the Diamond-D and Sheriff Cotton could only wonder what repercussions their deaths would have on his town. However, although his admonishment of Ethan Brodie was terse, he knew as well as Ethan that there was nothing else he could do, indeed, all anyone could do was await Luther Drummond's reaction.

While Ethan Brodie collected his gun that had been stored under the counter by the bartender, and while the rest of the room hummed with the excited conversation of those who had witnessed the killings and those who had been attracted to the Drover's Rope as a result of the gunplay, one man alone watched quietly as the bodies of the Collier brothers were carried off on boards to the undertaker's parlour. The man was Luke Taverner, Cal Collier's companion earlier that evening. Chilled by the death of his friend he went into the street, found his horse and set out to take the news to the Diamond-D.

12

While events unfolded in the Drover's Rope Saloon, Luther Drummond rode north. Two topics occupied his mind. First was the man Brodie. Shortly after he and the sheriff rode away from the Diamond-D ranch house, one of the young hands, Cal Collier had spoken up, told him he recognized Brodie from dealings he had when punching cows in New Mexico. Brodie was a Pinkerton man, Cal had told him, one of several employed to break the power of a local cattle baron. They succeeded, claiming the cattle baron had built his herd with rustled cattle. Men had been killed, Cal reported, but he hadn't offered up the fact that one of them was his brother.

The other topic which dominated his musing centred around his son. Dagg had been the centre of his life for nearly thirty years, ever since his wife had been carried off with a fever and the boy not yet two years old. Raising beeves was all Luther knew but he knew it better than most other men in Montana and building up the Diamond-D to be the biggest cattle spread in the state would prove that. It would also be his legacy to his son to whom, over the years, he tried pass on his knowledge. However, he had long accepted that Dagg had no affinity with the land nor any real attachment to raising cattle. Indeed, he had never shown skill at any aspect of ranching. Even with good people around him, such as the Dumbril girl, if she could have been persuaded to be his wife, and Gus Hardin as top hand, Luther suspected his son would be incapable of running the Diamond-D after he was gone. Indeed, Dagg had never displayed an aptitude for any kind of work or any individuality which proved him capable of an independent life. He needed his father and the security associated with his status at the

Diamond-D. With those facts in mind, earlier that year, Luther had made a decision which he revealed to no one. Not even Dagg whom it most affected.

Darkness had fallen long before Luther reached his destination. With a moonless sky, darkness on the open meadow was so complete that it was possible for a stranger to ride within fifty yards of the north meadow line shack and pass by without knowing of its existence. Luther Drummond knew it was there; he had built it, but, even so, the nicker of tethered horses who had caught the scent of his own, came as a mild surprise. The horses — there were three of them — were rope-tied to a picket line in front of the shack rather than loose in the corral at the back.

Luther heard the shack door open and the ratchet sound of a Winchester's mechanism as he stepped down from the saddle.

'Who's there,' someone called.

'Drummond.' His voice was a low

rumble which carried a hint of impatience.

'Pa.' Dagg spoke when Luther stepped inside. 'What are you doing here?'

Luther scanned the room. Two kerosene lamps on the rough table shed enough light for the card game he'd interrupted. Dagg was standing behind the table and Charlie Tyson, rifle still in his hands, stood near the door. Lou Petersen, fingering the silver pendant that hung from his gunbelt, remained seated at one side of the table. Three men, three horses. For a moment Luther enjoyed a sense of relief. 'Chad sitting the herd?' he asked.

In the corner there was a shuffling, someone stirred on a bunk. A voice spoke. 'I'm here, Mr Drummond.' Luther peered in that direction and lifted one of the lamps to cast light that way. The face he saw was pale, sickly looking, with purple and yellow marking around the raised lump on his brow and blackness around his left eye.

'What happened to you?'

Dagg answered for the wounded cowboy. 'His horse stumbled. He'll be OK.'

'What about the horse?'

Dagg grinned. 'You're worried about the horse?'

'There are only three out there.'

'Broke its leg. Had to be destroyed.' The story Dagg told was that the accident had occurred only that morning while rounding up strays along the northern ridge. He commended Chad for choosing to stay up at the line camp and told his pa that he'd planned to ride down to the ranch at daybreak to collect another mount for him.

Luther examined Chad's face again. The injuries seemed to be more than a day old but he wanted to believe his son. He sat down, accepted a mug of coffee from Charlie Tyson and regaled the four men with the details of the assault on Ethan Brodie, the hold-up of the Billings stagecoach and the death of Joe Dumbril and Siggi Larrsen. He explained that the horse taken from Ethan Brodie had been used in the hold-up and that the sheriff was looking for the same men for both crimes. 'There's talk that you four are the men involved.'

Dagg's temper flared. 'Who says that?'

'The descriptions this fellow Brodie gave fits, and it seems that Ellen Hartley can confirm his story.'

'Well it ain't true,' snapped Dagg. 'We've never been off Diamond-D range land.'

'There's a dead Diamond-D horse at the spot where the attack on Brodie is said to have happened. It's your horse, Dagg. The one you rode out on yesterday morning.'

'Can't be. My horse is tied to the picket line outside.'

'Gus rode over and took a look at it. He identified it.'

'Hardin,' snarled Dagg. 'You taking his word against your own son. He never did like me. Just been waiting his chance to make me look bad in your eyes.'

Dagg's words surprised Luther. The existence of bad blood between Gus and his son had never occurred to him. Over the years, Gus had shown more loyalty to himself and the Diamond-D brand than any man had reason to expect from a hired hand. But he recalled Gus's reluctance earlier in the day to acknowledge Dagg's innocence and, for the first time, he'd shown a hint of criticism at the order to kill Brodie if he returned to range land belonging to the Diamond-D. Perhaps, Luther thought, he was mistaken about Gus. Perhaps Dagg's failures as a cattleman had prompted ideas of becoming more than top hand. Dagg was the natural successor to inherit the ranch but a conviction for murder would change that. Identifying the dead horse as Dagg's would be telling evidence in a court of law. His mind jumped to thoughts of a conspiracy against his family, an association between Gus Hardin and the man Brodie who seemed hell-bent on making trouble. If Dagg was removed from the scene, Hardin, he suspected, envisaged a partnership then future ownership of the largest cattle empire in Montana. 'No,' he said. 'I'm not taking anyone's word against my son's. I told Bob Cotton he had no jurisdiction on this land and I told Brodie he'd be shot as a trespasser if he set foot on the Diamond-D again. But it may be better if none of you fellows go into Bridger Butte until the unrest that's hanging about the place has gone. I don't want you getting into trouble.'

Dagg queried his father's words. 'What trouble? Bob Cotton isn't going to come looking for me if he wants to keep his job.'

'Perhaps not,' said his pa, 'but Brodie sent a message for you to stay away from the Dumbril girl. Seems he's set himself up as her protector now that old Joe's dead.'

Unable to restrain his anger, Dagg

flung the cards he held across the room and ranted at his father for allowing a stranger to dictate terms to a Drummond. Such was his anger that he almost blurted out a wish that he hadn't been so lenient with the uppity stranger whose horse he'd taken. Forcing Lou, Chad and Charlie to stand knee deep in the river had already marked the man Brodie for some special attention on their next visit to town, but this insult wouldn't keep. No one told Dagg Drummond who he could or could not speak to.

Luther offered a piece of advice. 'I want you to stay away from Brodie.' His words were intended for everyone in the room. 'I'm told he's a Pinkerton man. I want no trouble with the Pinkertons until I find out why he's here and who brought him.'

Although he spoke no more of the matter that night, Dagg's temper simmered at a temperature just below boiling point. Assured that his pa's mind was now clear of all suspicion that he and his riding partners had had any part to play in the attacks on Brodie and the Billings stagecoach, he further duped him into believing that they wouldn't go into Bridger Butte until the furore over the deaths of Joe Dumbril and Siggi Larrsen had died down. In fact, he was determined to deal with the newcomer the next day. Somehow they would lure him on to Diamond-D land and kill him.

* * *

With thick black coffee in his stomach and the anticipation of flapjacks four hours away, Luther Drummond left the line shack as the first rays of the morning sun bled red across the pasture land. Forty minutes later, a pencil scrawled letter tucked deep inside the pocket of his shirt, Charlie Tyson saddled his cow pony and followed the same trail for some miles before veering westerly to the town of Bridger Butte. He was followed, an hour after that, by Dagg and Lou Petersen, leaving Chad Trelawney to handle a string of chores around the cabin.

Ethan Brodie didn't take breakfast at his sister's house, choosing instead to take a plate of bacon and eggs at the eating house he'd used before yesterday's funeral. The previous night he'd sensed the disapproval of his sister and her husband when he'd told them of the violence at the Drover's Rope and his part in it. Claire Dumbril had already retired to her room and spent the night in ignorance of the killing of the Collier brothers. At first light Ethan had been astir and, rather than disturb the sleeping household, had gone abroad in search of breakfast and a livery horse.

Contrary to the threat of being shot if he trespassed on Diamond-D land, Ethan's intention this day was to ride north to see if he could find and identify those riders who had attacked him and stolen his horse. Given the

203

opportunity, he would have liked to have been accompanied by Bob Cotton. No matter how much Luther Drummond proclaimed himself emperor of this part of Montana, the presence of the lawman would probably prevent indiscriminate violence by any of his cowboys. In addition, it would be a sign to Ethan that the sheriff cared about bringing to justice those responsible for the deaths of Joe Dumbril and Siggi Larrsen. However, given the sheriff's declared reluctance to pursue any crime beyond the town limits and his clear warning to Ethan to steer clear of involvement with Drummond's riders, Ethan saw no value in telling the lawman his plans.

Ethan's first stop was the livery stable where he checked out the well-being of his distinctive stallion. The stable owner, a stocky man with a moustache like a paint brush approached. 'You the one who caused the ruckus last night?' Ethan moved his head in a single nod, cautious as to the man's purpose.

'Funny thing,' the stableman said, 'never knew those Collier boys to cause trouble before.'

'Wasn't the way I wanted it,' said Ethan.

'So I was told. Seems Drummond had all his boys het up. They've gone now, though. All the Diamond-D boys left town after the shooting.' He shook his head. 'Such a pity,' he added.

Ethan wondered if the stableman's mutterings were heading somewhere. 'Still OK to leave my horse here?' he asked.

The man looked at him. 'Sure,' he said. 'Still fifty cents a day like we agreed. No more, no less. I liked young Cal. And Fitz, but if two guns go up against an unarmed man you can't have any sympathy for them if they wind up dead.'

'Guess not,' said Ethan, happy enough to agree. 'I need to hire a good horse for the day. Won't be racing it but it will need stamina. What have you got?' After settling on a chestnut gelding Ethan asked to have it ready for ten o'clock then went off to tackle breakfast at the eating house.

Ethan was leaning against a post at the corner of the sidewalk outside the eating house watching the town come to life. Sunday morning, and though he knew there was no church building in Bridger Butte, Ethan sussed there had to be some sort of meeting place at the west end of Drover Street. Men, women and young'uns, most with washed faces and catalogue clothes, passed by in buggies and afoot, faces full of smiles and goodwill. Among the citizens making their way to the Sunday Meeting were his sister and her husband. Irene inquired if he would be joining them at the hymn singing but Ethan declined. He had something to check out, he told them, but didn't go into detail. Didn't tell them that he planned to search Drummond land for the men who had stolen his horse.

After Irene and Jim had moved on, a young lad came at a run and stopped in front of Ethan. 'Mr Brodie, sir?' the boy inquired, but held out an envelope with more certainty than was in his voice. Ethan could see his name scrawled on the envelope in pencil as he took it from the boy who then ran back along the street in the direction from which he'd come. Ethan withdrew the single sheet. On it was written one sentence: 'If you want to find those who held up the stage,' it read, 'come to the grove above Whitefish Brook'.

The boy was out sight, unavailable to tell Ethan either the identity of the person who had asked him to deliver it or the location of Whitefish Brook. The answer to the second question, how-ever, was easily obtained.

'That's on Drummond land now,' the stableman told him when he went to collect the gelding. 'Used to be Johnny Harper's until he was forced to sell up. Keep to this side of the river until you've passed the cascade. Mile or so after that you'll be able to see the crossing point. Once you're on the other side head over the foothills. You'll see Johnny's burned out house off to your left. From there you can make Whitefish Brook in ten minutes at a canter.'

Ethan was under no illusion about the message. The probability that it was a trap was apparent but, in keeping with his usual *modus operandi*, he was prepared to take the bull by the horns and follow where clues led. Checking first that his six-gun and Winchester were fully loaded, he stepped up into the saddle and rode north.

At that moment a man on a chestnut mare appeared at the south end of Drover Street. He was dusty and hot and had clearly travelled far, but his attire, though casual, was of better quality than that of a saddle tramp or cattle worker. He wore dark cord trousers, a white cotton shirt and, around his collar, a slim ribbon of black silk tied in a neat, even bow. His sand coloured hair was well groomed and his slim moustache was trimmed.

When he dismounted at the livery stable, the stableman grabbed the reins to lead the horse into a stall. 'Staying long, mister?'

'One night. Horse and I both need a rest.'

'Come far?'

'Billings.'

'Butte Hotel is the best place in town. Two dollars a night. Fifty cents here for your horse.'

'Sounds fair,' said the man and he dug in a trouser pocket to find the necessary coins. 'I need to ride out to the Diamond-D ranch shortly,' he said. 'I'd prefer to make the trip in a little more comfort. A buggy would suit me fine.'

'Got one out back,' said the stableman. 'Cost you two dollars for the afternoon. Bring back a sound horse and an undamaged vehicle and you'll get one back.' He ended his sales pitch with a curt nod of the head to indicate that the man was getting the best of the agreement.

* * *

The directions Ethan had been given were easy to follow, the trail to the river crossing was flat and the horse he had under him felt strong and eager. The day was hot, as it had been when he'd first arrived in Bridger Butte, the sky was blue and the green meadow stretched endlessly before him. Restlessly, he gazed at the snow topped Bitterroots, knowing that Idaho and Oregon, states he had never visited, lay beyond.

Crossing the river concentrated his mind on the task in hand. He knew that if he was being led into a trap it would take place on the eastern bank, range which belonged to Luther Drummond. Even if this wasn't a deliberate trap the very fact that he was riding on Diamond-D land put his life at risk. Judging by last night's gunplay, Luther Drummond's hired hands were only too willing to back up their boss's threats.

He urged the gelding into a canter as they tackled the slopes away from the river and, at the summit, in a clearing to his left, he espied the ruined ranch house that had once been Johnny Harper's home. He halted, scanned the land before him and withdrew his Winchester from its boot. He worked the mechanism so that it was primed for firing then carried it, butt resting on his right thigh, as he pricked the beast's flanks with his spurs.

Casting looks all around, he proceeded at a walk. At one moment he thought he saw movement among the pines on the slopes above him. He halted. Waited and watched, but there was no repetition. He moved on, slowly, approaching the small body of water which he guessed was Whitefish Brook. Beyond that, about quarter of a mile distant, he could see a cluster of trees which he assumed was the grove mentioned in the message. The two hundred yard trail leading up to it was the perfect setting for an ambush, being both a progressive incline and a one-sided gully. It followed the curve of a low mound to the left but, to the right, the land rose abruptly thus being unusable as an avenue of escape. Anyone on the trail under fire from the mound to the left would be trapped.

Ethan dismounted and ground tied the gelding near the water. If he was walking into a trap he was probably already under surveillance. His best chance was to make himself as small a target as possible and move quickly. With a last quick survey of the grove at the top of the hill, he set off, keeping to the high ground to the right of the trail. Crouching as he ran he got to within fifty yards of the grove. Here, the trail below swung to the left as it circled the mound. He paused, stood taller to permit himself a fuller view of the grove and at that moment it registered that a man with a rifle was aiming at him from the summit of the low mound across the trail. The instinctive need to react meant that his sighting of the gunman was nothing more than momentary. Even so, the slimness of the figure made him unmistakable. It was a man Ethan had last seen standing knee deep in the Dearborn, a man from whose gunbelt dangled a silver medallion.

Ethan dropped to the ground and rolled as a first bullet hissed over his body and a second kicked up dirt where he had hit the ground. Such was the angle of incline where he'd fallen that his momentum made it impossible to stop the roll and bullets were whining past him as he headed for the drop on to the trail. Two thoughts lodged in his mind as he rolled, neither of them provided comfort. First, he knew that when he hit the trail he would come to a full stop and he would be an easy target for the gunman. The second thought was that there were so many bullets zinging around him that there was more than one man firing at him.

Instinct had caused him to hang on to his rifle but he was unable to fire off a single shot, yet, as he hurtled towards the drop on to the trail he thought he heard a cry of pain from one of his assailants. But even as that thought entered his mind he dropped into the gully and the breath was forced from his body. He scrambled to his knees, expecting every second to be his last. But no gunman appeared above him to fire the final bullet and gradually he realized that the gunfire he could hear was coming from the slope behind him, not from the mound in front. He gripped his rifle and raised his head. Whoever had waited in ambush had gone. He turned his attention to the high ground down which he'd fallen. A figure, rifle at the ready, was coming down the hillside to join him. When she was within five paces of him, Claire Dumbril asked, 'Are you hit, Ethan?'

13

Apart from a sore left shoulder which had taken the main force of impact with the ground, Ethan was unscathed. As they walked back to the brook where Ethan had tethered his horse, Claire recounted how she had watched his curious behaviour from the cover of the trees high on the ridge above. She had caught the movement of those who waited in ambush mere seconds before they'd taken their first shots at him but, as she'd left the town with the intention of bringing fresh meat to the Claymores' table, her rifle was primed and handy when the attack began. To Ethan's benefit, her marksmanship was good. He learned that she'd hunted game all her life and had been out hunting the day he'd arrived in Bridger Butte. He remembered the blood on her hands and clothing when he'd first seen her in the jailhouse.

She had counted three men shooting from the mound across the trail, one of them she'd hit and another she'd recognized as Dagg Drummond. They had hightailed it when their gunfire was returned, presumably because they hadn't known who or how many were shooting at them. However, judging by the way Ethan had gone down under the first volley, it was possible they'd gone because they thought they had killed their quarry. Claire, herself, had feared as much. The relief she'd felt when he'd stood up un-bloodied had taken her by surprise. So, too, had his smile. It seemed to carry more meaning than just gratitude for the rescue.

They'd climbed the mound, found a few spent cartridge shells and could see a wisp of the dust being kicked up by the departing riders as they travelled north. Claire was curious as to why Ethan had come on to this stretch of Drummond range. When he showed her the note he'd received she immediately identified Dagg Drummond's writing. 'Good thing I changed my plans,' she said. 'I usually go over by the Big Timbers to hunt. I guess my mind is fixed on Pa at the moment. And Johnny.' She glanced at Ethan to gauge his reaction to mention of her fiancé's name. 'I used to come here when Johnny owned the land. This is where we'd hoped to live. He vowed that one day he'd return and buy back this spread. The last time I saw him was back at the ruins of his house. He promised to rebuild it for me; bigger and better than it had been before the fire. We exchanged gifts. He gave me this.' She pushed up the right sleeve of her rough shirt. Around her wrist was a bracelet of stones and shells, an Indian ornament that was full of colour and delicacy. 'I gave him a pendant. A silver disc on a thong to hang around his neck. It wasn't expensive.' She shrugged and smiled, mainly a comfort to herself. 'It was etched with the head of an eagle. He was so happy with it,' she said. The smile on her face disappeared. The worry and anger that Ethan had first seen in Bob Cotton's office two days earlier, settled across her features again. The blue of her eyes darkened almost to black. 'I know if it was possible,' she said, 'that he would have been in touch with me. The fact that he hasn't convinces me that he's dead.'

At Whitefish Brook she climbed up behind him and they rode up to the high ground where Claire had left her own horse when the shooting began. They spoke little on the short journey, Ethan pleasantly aware of the closeness of the girl behind. And there were other thoughts in his mind. First, the disc Claire had described. He remembered the one that had been tied around the gunbelt that he'd taken from the tall man when he'd forced him into the river. It, too, had been etched with an eagle's head. For the moment, he kept the information to himself.

He thought also of the note Dagg

Drummond had sent. As a location for an ambush it couldn't be faulted. If Claire hadn't been on hand it was most likely that he would now be dead. But why had this isolated spot been chosen? Luther Drummond was so confident of his position as ruler of this territory that he had openly declared a death sentence on Ethan if he trespassed on their land so, once across the river, his life was already forfeit. There was no need to hide the fact of his killing. Indeed, to prove his power, it was more likely that Luther would want news of his death broadcast to the citizens of Bridger Butte and beyond. So why choose such a specific location?

Ethan's answer to his own question was that Dagg wanted to be sure that he had no chance of outrunning his attackers on the open plain, he wanted to be certain of a killing and to that end had chosen a place which had proved successful in the past. If Ethan was right, the need then had not only been to hide the fact of the killing but also the body. From the view from the top of the ridge the grove of two dozen trees which had been specified in the note appeared to be a suitable location.

Once remounted on her own mare Ethan asked Claire to ride into town and report the shooting to the sheriff. 'What are you going to do?' she asked.

'Try to find them,' he lied. Claire wanted to ride with him but he insisted she went into Bridger Butte. As much as he enjoyed having her near, if he found what he was really going to look for, she was the last person he wanted with him. He watched her almost down to the brook before riding off in the opposite direction, down to the grove.

The grove, a stand of cottonwoods and ash trees covered almost an acre of land. The old trees with their twisted trunks and spreading branches provided a cool, shaded place both in which to picket the livery horse and to search for a grave. The latter wasn't difficult to find, his killers no doubt, confident in the fact that it was on land that would never be searched by any law officer. The body hadn't been put underground, merely covered with a gathering of branches and stones forming a pile that stood out like a fully plumed Cheyenne war chief in a Boston saloon.

Ethan was examining the decomposing body — there were three bullet holes in the head — when a swift, fluttered whinny from his horse alerted him to the fact that he was not alone. He turned, swiftly, his hand reaching for his hand gun, but the figure behind him was no threat.

'You didn't ride north,' Claire said. 'I came to see what you're looking for here.' Ethan stepped in front of her, gripped her shoulders, tried to turn her away from where the body lay, but she struggled, tried to look over his shoulder, her curiosity piqued by his behaviour. She asked the question. 'What have you found?'

He held her at arms length. Held her eyes. Said the words as gently as he was able, knowing that gentle or rough the words would crush her world. 'It's Johnny.'

There was the slightest catch in her throat, a gasp that was so soft and stifled that it could have been nothing more than a breeze moving a leaf of the overhanging cottonwood. But his hands were still on her shoulders and he felt the tremor that passed through her. She moved to step around him. His instinct was to prevent her from seeing the decaying body of the man she had intended to marry, but that was only a momentary reaction. Instead, understanding that nothing hastens the acceptance of a death more than viewing the body, he took her by the left arm and stayed beside her while she looked on the fractured, withering face of the man who had once been Johnny Harper. Without tears or any outward display of anger she knelt beside the corpse. Ethan watched her with a mixture of sympathy and admiration. When he'd fetched a blanket from the bundle tied behind his saddle he placed it over Johnny's head and fixed it in place with some of the stones that had been piled over him. 'Someone will answer for this,' he told Claire. When she looked into his eyes she knew it was a promise he would keep.

★　★　★

Only once before had Luther Drummond met the neat man who stepped down from the buggy at the ranch house door. That had been in Billings, gathered around a desk in a first floor room of the Cattlemen's Bank. His name was Walt Benning, a man with a polished exterior who said little but watched and listened like a buzzard two arms' length away from a dying man. There had been three other people present that day: Hec Bishop, Vice-president in charge of that bank's interests in Montana, and Henry Pardew and Ambrose Carpenter, senior partners in a New York Investment syndicate seeking to establish an equivalent stock breeding concern in this northern state to the one that thrived in New Mexico. It was the final week of February and the full cost of the winter catastrophe was only just apparent to Luther. Hec Bishop had first approached him two weeks earlier, making an offer for the Diamond-D on behalf of the syndicate, an offer which was well below Luther's estimation. But the winter losses, his son's limitations and negotiations around a more realistic figure had encouraged him to sell the land, the stock and the brand. The sale remained a secret between the interested parties. Even Dagg was unaware that he would never inherit the vast acreage of the Diamond-D.

All that had mattered to Luther Drummond for most of the last thirty years was raising cattle and his son. Until recently he had thought the two things inseparable but recently he had acknowledged that his dream of passing on a cattle empire to future generations of Drummonds would never become reality. Even so, although the sale of the

Diamond-D had realized enough money to take him anywhere in the world, raising cattle was all that Luther knew. He couldn't envisage life for himself anywhere but on the open range of the Montana cattle land. Accordingly, as part of the deal, he stayed on to run the ranch on behalf of the syndicate. For their part, the syndicate tempered this concession by charging him with the task of increasing the land mass under their control, a bonus payable for every small ranch that he could annex to the Diamond-D.

Walt Benning kept an office in Billings for the syndicate. Luther reported to him once a month and it was through him that syndicate money was made available for the purchase of adjoining ranches. He was also the man appointed to take control of the Diamond-D if the syndicate ever deemed it necessary. When Luther saw the sharp-eyed man step out of the buggy, he felt a sudden tightness in his throat, and when refreshment of any kind was refused he experienced a tension of dreadful expectation akin to that which he'd known the night a band of Arapaho had besieged his original cabin.

They stood in the centre of the large room where ranch business was carried out, Walt Benning's words cutting as deeply into Luther as any Indian hatchet ever could. The money entrusted to him for the purchase of Siggi Larrsen's land had found its way back to the Cattleman's Bank, still bound in that bank's identifying wrappers, and put into a new account opened by Dagg Drummond. An inquisitive teller who checked the serial numbers with those issued to Walt Benning reported the deposit to Hec Bishop. He, familiar with the syndicate's purpose for the earlier withdrawal of the cash, connected it with the telegraphed news of the stage hold-up and the murder of Siggi Larrsen. Walt, on behalf of the syndicate, wanted an explanation.

Dumbfounded by the news, numbed by the dawning realization that Dagg had lied to him, Luther struggled to form any sort of coherent answer.

'I'm here to give you a few hours' head start on the law,' said Walt Benning. 'The syndicate can't be associated with such crimes as murder and highway robbery. You and your son had best head out of Montana immediately. Hec Bishop is holding off reporting the deposit of the stolen money until tomorrow morning. When he does I expect the federal marshal will make a beeline for this place.'

'I had nothing to do with it,' Luther said hopelessly. 'You can have the money back. If the bank doesn't report it no one will ever know about Dagg's involvement. No one in Bridger Butte will testify against him.' Even as the words left his mouth he pictured the assured rider who'd looked down at him the day before and threatened his son. And that thought was crowded by the image of Luke Taverner's vivid account of the killing of the Collier brothers and his insistence that Ellen Hartley could identify the riders who had stolen Brodie's horse. He'd dismissed Luke Taverner's talk when he'd spoken to him in the corral but, at that time, he'd been prepared to believe his son was innocent. Now, of all the citizens around Bridger Butte, Ellen Hartley was the one who considered herself on equal footing with the Drummonds. If she believed Dagg was guilty he had no doubt that she would testify to the fact.

Walt Benning's voice cut through his deliberation. 'Makes no difference. Henry Pardew is running for governor. He can't afford to have anything unsavoury attached to him or his business dealings. In a way, you're lucky he's given you the benefit of an advance warning. It could only be to his political advantage to be seen to be instrumental in the arrest of a murderer and robber. If I were you I'd make every minute he's given you count. But, come what may,' he added, 'be gone by this time tomorrow. When I return I'll be in charge of the Diamond-D.'

14

Up to the moment they'd come under fire from the top of the opposite ridge, Dagg's ambush had gone according to plan. The threesome had watched Brodie almost from the moment he'd crossed the river. Hitching his horse near Whitefish Brook had surprised them but, as a target, he was no more difficult to hit scampering afoot on the steep slope than riding up the trail to the grove. Lou Petersen was less than thirty paces from Ethan when he stepped into view, rifle rising to his shoulder, grinning with anticipation, certain that the indignity of standing knee deep in the water of the Dearborn was about to be repaid with interest. He paused momentarily, long enough to be sure that Ethan Brodie recognized him then squeezed the trigger. Through the rising smoke he saw his quarry go down, roll forward, down the incline, gathering momentum until he crashed into the gully.

Charlie Tyson shouted. 'You got him, Lou,' and stepped forward firing shot after shot at the rolling figure, eager for Ethan to fall into the gully knowing that when he did he would be defenceless, totally at the mercy of his adversaries and knowing that none would be shown. Then the first shot had come from the top of the ridge. It hit Charlie in the guts and came out the back with a squelch of blood and tissue. The force of the impact spun him around so that, as his legs buckled, unwittingly, he staggered back towards the cover from which he'd emerged.

More shots followed, whizzing too close to Lou and Dagg for them to remain in the open. Unable to see or count those who were shooting at them they took to the cover of the rocks among which they'd waited to ambush Ethan. They were surprised by this turn of events, convinced that he'd been alone when he'd approached Whitefish Brook. Whoever was shooting at them must have crossed the river at a lower point and circled around to give him protection while he made a bold frontal approach. Dagg guessed it was Bob Cotton. If so, it was likely that he would challenge Dagg and his partners to put up their arms. When this didn't happen and a couple more shots splintered stone near his head, he signalled to Lou to head for their tethered horses. Between them, they dragged the bloodied Charlie Tyson and flung him across his saddle. Charlie, pallid, face contorted with pain, made little protest and little noise as they galloped away.

They rode north for two miles, Dagg throwing occasional glances back across the pasture land for signs of pursuit and Lou holding the reins of Charlie's horse to make sure it didn't run off on a trail of its own. Eventually, Lou called for a halt and stepped down to examine the unconscious Charlie Tyson who was draped over the saddle as though he was already dead. 'No good carrying on to the line shack if you want to keep Charlie alive,' he declared. 'He needs a doctor. Needs one quick.'

Dagg hadn't dismounted. His gaze was fixed on their back trail while Lou assessed Charlie's condition. He wasn't surprised by the lack of pursuit. Charlie had been adamant that Lou had got Brodie when he'd opened fire at him across the trail. Brodie had been warned not to stray on to Drummond territory, everyone knew that, so if he ended up dead it was his own fault. Bob Cotton might protest about the killing but there wasn't anything he could do about it — the Drummonds ruled on the Diamond-D. 'We'll take him back to the ranch,' he said. 'I'll tell Pa that Brodie fired the first shot. That we had no alternative but to fight back. He'll believe me and dismiss any stories he hears to the contrary as rumours put about by disgruntled townsfolk jealous of the power of the Drummonds.'

So they turned around and, travelling

more slowly, returned to the Diamond-D ranch house. There was no sign of activity around the trail from Whitefish Brook where the gunfight had occurred, but they didn't dally there, confident that whoever had come to Ethan Brodie's aid had collected his body and taken it back to Bridger Butte. Perhaps under other circumstances, if they hadn't been toting a wounded man or if Dagg hadn't been certain that Ethan Brodie was dead, they might have cast more than a cursory glance in the direction of the grove and they might have caught the movement of grazing horses or a man shifting rubble. But they didn't. Oblivious of Ethan and Claire's discovery of Johnny Harper's body, they rode steadily south.

A man driving a one-horse buggy came under the swinging sign of the Diamond-D as Dagg, Lou and the unconscious Charlie Tyson approached. He wore a stern expression as he passed the trio, his interest in the body draped over the third horse causing him to look back as the vehicle rattled by. For a moment it seemed that he would drive on, then, with a hard jerk of the reins, he hauled the horse to a halt before circling back to the riders. 'What happened?' he asked.

'What business is it of yours?' Dagg asked.

'Does he ride for the Diamond-D?'

'Yes.'

'Then it's my business.'

Dagg straightened in the saddle, his lips curled into a snarl of anger. 'I don't know who you are, mister, but the Diamond-D is Drummond land and what happens here is only the business of the Drummonds.'

Walt Benning studied the angry face before him. 'Are you Dagg Drummond?'

'What of it?'

'There have been changes. I'm the boss of the Diamond-D.' Dagg's look of disbelief prompted him to add more. 'Check with your father,' he said, 'but first tell me what happened to that man. Is he dead?'

In response to the stranger's question Lou Petersen bent down from the saddle to inspect Charlie. It took only a moment to decide. 'Reckon he is.' Dagg was gazing towards the ranch house where he could see the figure of his father on the porch. Bewildered by the stranger's words and stunned by the emphatic manner in which he'd declared himself the boss of the Diamond-D, Dagg found himself unable to speak. Lou took it upon himself to answer the man's question, sticking to the story that Dagg had proposed. 'We got ambushed. A saddle tramp who's been making trouble for the Diamond-D. A man called Ethan Brodie. But he won't trouble us no more.'

'Ethan Brodie! The Pinkerton man?'

'Pinkerton?' The word brought Dagg back into the conversation.

'The Ethan Brodie I know works for the Pinkerton Agency,' confirmed Walt Benning.

'This guy doesn't work for anybody anymore,' Lou said.

'You've killed him? You've killed Ethan Brodie?'

'He ambushed us,' Dagg snapped. 'He got what he deserved.'

The message in the long, steel-eyed look that Walt Benning gave to Dagg Drummond indicated precisely what he thought of Dagg's explanation. If the man who'd been killed was the same Ethan Brodie that the Pinkerton Agency had sent to investigate the cattle losses on the syndicate's New Mexico ranch, then attacking men from ambush was not part of his character. It was more likely that the perpetration of an ambush had been used against him. 'Best get that man laid out for burial,' he told Lou Petersen, 'and you,' he turned his attention to the furrow-browed Dagg, 'go speak to your father.' With those words he clicked his tongue and slapped the leathers over the rump of his horse, starting it on the trail back to Bridger Butte.

Amid a lot of questions, ranch-hands helped Lou Petersen get Charlie Tyson's body to the bunk house. Meanwhile, Dagg confronted his father. It was a heated exchange; Luther, distraught though he was by the fact that his son was a robber and a killer, couldn't hide his anger that his son's actions were driving him away from the land he loved; and Dagg, stunned by the revelation that Luther had sold the Diamond-D months earlier blamed his father for caring more about cattle than he did his son. Even though Dagg had long accepted that he was not cut out for ranch life, the knowledge that his father had no faith in his ability to run the Diamond-D was a bitter pill to swallow. Nor was it tempered by the fact that a sum of money far in excess of what he needed to finance his business plan sat in a Drummond account at the Cattleman's Bank. Just a fraction of that money which, one day, would all be his, would have been enough to take him to San Francisco where he could have studied photography and established a studio and camera store. Luther's plea that he had had no idea that his son wanted to leave the ranch brought a hollow laugh from Dagg. 'Apart from knowing what I can't do,' Dagg accused his father, 'you've never tried to find out what I can do.'

In ignorance of the available money, Dagg had taken what had been paid to Siggi Larrsen. Now he regretted not going immediately to San Francisco. If he'd deposited the money in a bank there instead of Billings, the current situation would never have arisen. But in the morning the law would learn of his involvement with the hold-up of the stagecoach and State officers would come for him. He knew they'd dig deep enough to learn that he'd robbed and killed Johnny Harper, too.

'Listen,' said Luther, the heat of recrimination cooling, the need for a resolution to secure his son's safety dominant. 'Perhaps I can persuade the bank to keep their information to themselves. After all, they can have the money that you deposited. We don't need to make mention of it again. And if that cowboy, Brodie is dead who is there to testify against you?'

'Benning said that Brodie is a Pinkerton man,' Dagg reminded his father.

'Pinkerton man or saddle tramp. What's the difference if he's dead?'

'What about Bob Cotton? If he shot Charlie Tyson, he knows it was Lou and I who killed Brodie.'

'So what. As far as Bob Cotton knows this is still our land. You stick to the story that Brodie fired first and there's no case to answer.' Luther grinned at his son, confidence seeping back into his spirit. Then a thought struck. 'Ellen Hartley,' he said. 'She might make trouble. She knows it was you who rode away to Gunner Pass. But perhaps we can do something about that. Come on, son. Let's pay a visit to our neighbours.'

★   ★   ★

When they left the grove, Claire and Ethan steered clear of the gully trail and rode to the top of the escarpment from where Claire had fired at Ethan's attackers. Claire knew another, less used, river crossing which would take ten minutes off the journey back to town. Looking south from the ridge, Claire pointed out three moving shapes about a mile distant. 'That's Dagg Drummond,' she declared, her voice low, certain, dangerous.

'I'm going after them,' said Ethan.

'We're going after them.'

'No,' argued Ethan. 'You go to town. Tell the sheriff everything and get him to come out to the Diamond-D. I won't do anything until he gets there.'

'No.' Claire was determined. 'This is my fight more than yours. If you're going to the Diamond-D then so am I.'

Ethan tried again. 'You brought me to Bridger Butte because you wanted my help.'

'Then help,' she told him, adamant that she would have her way, 'but you're not tackling them alone.'

'I don't want you hurt,' he told her,

his voice gentler, the implication undisguised.

'I don't want you hurt either.' Her eyes held his, her chin jutted slightly forward, daring him to reject the affection she was offering. The tension in her body manifested itself in a slight tremble.

He reached forward and covered the hand that rested on the saddle horn with his own. 'Come on then,' he said, and they set off in pursuit.

Fifteen minutes later, their mounts blowing hard from the exertion of closing the gap to little more than four hundred yards, they paused in the cover of some cottonwoods on a rise looking down on the Diamond-D compound. Dagg and his slim companion were in conversation with a man driving a one horse buggy. The man slung over the third horse seemed to be the topic of conversation. After a moment the buggy set along the trail to Bridger Butte while the horsemen galloped through the gateway towards the ranch house.

Ethan kept his eyes on the buggy and, selecting a route which would keep them from sight of anyone watching from the ranch, rode into the road to intercept it.

'I'm seeing a ghost.' Walt Benning had a grin on his face.

'I thought I recognized you, Walt,' said Ethan, 'And what do you mean, a ghost?'

'Just spoken to a man who claims he killed you. Thwarted your attempted ambush and killed you instead.'

'Something twisted about that story, Walt, but they came mighty close to killing me. Would have done it, too, if Miss Dumbril hadn't been on hand.'

Walt Benning tipped his hat at Claire. The fact that she had no smile to offer in return had nothing to do with any connection he might have with the Drummond family, all to do with the circumstances that had brought her to this moment. 'The ambush was set by Dagg Drummond,' she said. 'He lured Ethan into it.' Her mouth set again in a thin line of tension.

'I never figured it any other way, Miss Dumbril.'

'What are you doing here, Walt?' Ethan asked.

'Business. The same syndicate that hired you in New Mexico now owns the Diamond-D. Has done for several months.'

Ethan and Claire exchanged glances. It was Claire who asked for clarification. 'This isn't Drummond land?'

'No. Although I don't think Dagg knew that until I spoke to him. Dare say he's checking what I told him with Luther right now.'

Ethan related the story of the ambush to Walt Benning and gave him the note in Dagg's hand as proof of the plot. He also told him of the discovery of Johnny Harper's body and asked him to pass the information on to Sheriff Cotton. Just as they were about to part company they heard a drumming of hoof beats from the direction of the Diamond-D. Claire rode forward a little way to investigate. 'It's Luther, Dagg and that slim man,' she reported. 'They've gone west along the river. Towards the south crossing.'

15

Ever since the brief confrontation with Dagg Drummond down at the Dearborn, John Hartley had been uneasy. Over and over he'd recalled their conversation, knowing full well that it wasn't the words that unsettled him but the manner in which they'd been spoken and the insinuation behind them. Last night, if Ellen had been home, he'd have told her he was in favour of selling the ranch to Luther Drummond for a fair price. He wasn't afraid of hard work, indeed he would work all the hours necessary to make the ranch profitable and keep his wife comfortable, but he saw no sense in fighting. What would they be fighting for? There was no offspring to inherit the land. Better to make money from what they'd achieved now and pursue their lives somewhere else, than die here with no reward for their effort. Ellen would argue about that. This land was her life, and though she wouldn't say as much, she would translate selling out to the Drummonds as the act of a coward, not that of a practical man. She would bear arms herself against anyone who tried to usurp her, and he knew she would persuade him to stay even though the very thought of violence sickened him. He'd seen enough of that in the war; joining the Union army during the last years he'd soon discovered there was no romance or glory on a battlefield. Nonetheless, this day, John Hartley worked uneasily in the hayloft, his mind still wrestling with the desire to speak to his wife about selling up whenever she returned from her sister's homestead at the Big Timbers.

When he heard the riders clatter around the water trough in front of the ranch house, he lay aside the pitch fork, wiped the sleeve of his denim shirt across his brow and presented himself at the open top doors. Despite his mind being occupied by thoughts of the Drummonds, their presence in his compound startled him. John couldn't remember Luther Drummond visiting the ranch since the day he and Ellen married. Yet there he was. Dagg, too. Father and son, astride their mounts watching the door of his home, hands crossed carefully on their saddle horns, leaning slightly forward, suggestive of impatience, as though their arrival at a neighbour's home warranted instant attention. Behind them, Lou Petersen sat upright in his saddle, prepared for action, even, John thought, anxious for action, but cautious, too, his right hand flat on his thigh near his holstered Colt.

John noted their weaponry. All carried sidearms and a rifle in a saddle boot. Nothing unusual in that for since the war, few cowboys rode around without some form of firearm. Indeed, he carried a pistol himself when he was out on the range to use against snakes and marauding wolves. But, coupled with the suspicions with which his mind was aggravated, their militia-like appearance made John wary of their purpose. As was his usual practice when working around the ranch, he'd left his gunbelt in the house. It was often an impediment, especially so when forking hay. However, such had been his state of mind that morning he had brought with him his Winchester which he'd propped near the door frame against which he now leaned. For a moment he considered picking it up but it wasn't courteous to greet neighbours with a gun in hand. He pushed the door further open and called across the yard. 'Looking for me, Mr Drummond?'

The three riders turned their heads in the direction of the voice, then turned their horses. Using their knees they urged them forward a couple of slow, lazy strides. 'Come to make an offer for your ranch, Hartley. Good offer. Top price,' called Luther Drummond.

'Ranch isn't mine to sell,' John replied. 'You know that. It's Ellen's property and I don't expect she'll sell it to you.'

Lou Petersen moved his horse forward, edging between Luther and Dagg, giving himself a full view of John in the open doorway. Luther rubbed his jaw. 'Expect you can persuade her to see things different. You get her to accept my price and I'll see that a sum of money comes your way. Your own money, Hartley. Money you won't have to ask permission to use. Seems wrong to me that a man has no say in how his money should be spent.'

The insult, for such it was and meant to needle John Hartley into proving he was the master of affairs on this cattle spread, had the opposite effect to what Luther Drummond intended. Dagg Drummond smirked as he muttered a remark to Lou Petersen, his voice too low for the words to carry up to John Hartley, but John didn't need to hear them. He guessed they were in similar vein, a denigration of his position as Ellen's spouse. At that moment he realized that if people considered him an inferior partner in the running of the ranch it was because of his own reluctance to present himself as anything other than the hired hand who first arrived at Bridger Butte. Ellen was blameless for the impression he gave to the people of the area, she consulted him on all aspects of the ranch, and if he did defer to her wishes it was more to do with their compatibility than any conscious thought that the land had been bequeathed by her parents. He spoke sternly, determination replacing his normal pacifism. 'This ranch isn't for sale. If that's all you wanted I've got work to get on with.'

'I need this land, Hartley,' Luther called. 'Like I say, I'll pay top price. Top price for land and stock. But I want you off by the end of the week.'

'We're going nowhere,' John retorted, anger growing at Luther Drummond's resistance. 'Now get off my property.'

Lou Petersen's hand moved slowly until it covered the butt of his Colt. He spoke in a low voice, his lips barely moving. 'I can take him with one shot,' he told Luther.

Luther sat motionless, his mind a morass of conflict. He'd killed men in the past, but only to protect his land or his stock. He'd used a few dirty tactics recently to enable the annexation of land to the Diamond-D but killing the owners had never been part of the plan. He'd have paid a good price if they'd been willing to sell. But now his son's future was at stake. His only hope of preventing him facing a charge of murder was by persuading the bank that there was nothing to be gained by reporting the deposit of the money paid to Siggi Larrsen and the only way of achieving that was by removing any other evidence pointing to Dagg's guilt. According to his son, Ethan Brodie was already dead, which meant that the Hartleys were the last remaining threat. If they were gone from the area Dagg's name would be untarnished. He could go where he would and he, Luther, would give him whatever money he needed to start his new life. Still, however, he baulked at ordering Lou Petersen to shoot John Hartley.

The rattle of an approaching vehicle drew everyone's attention. Doc Priestpole's one horse buggy came into view from the far side of the house and in the seat beside the medical man was Ellen Hartley. The aura of confrontation escaped neither of the newcomers as they identified the riders. Ellen stepped down from the buggy and approached the riders. 'Mr Drummond,' she said by way of greeting. She looked at Dagg and Lou Petersen in turn without showing any mark of friendship or welcome.

'Mr Drummond wants to buy our ranch,' John called. 'I told him it's not for sale.'

Even though her husband's defiant words filled her with pride, Ellen Hartley didn't smile when she echoed his statement. 'That's right. This land is not for sale. Not to anyone,' she said, turning her face from Luther to Dagg and back again, 'and especially not to the Drummonds.'

Desperate, Luther tried again make a tempting offer. 'I'll pay top dollar — ' He began, but the sound of fast approaching horses interrupted his words. The appearance of Ethan Brodie and Claire Dumbril brought a muttering of curses from Dagg Drummond. Lou Petersen began to pull his Colt from the holster until Claire Dumbril, who had withdrawn her rifle approaching the Hartley's homestead, moved it threateningly in his direction.

Ellen Hartley was the first to speak, answering the offer that Luther Drummond had been in the process of declaring. 'Top dollar,' she stated, 'like the top dollar you paid Siggi Larrsen for his land.'

'I paid Siggi Larrsen a good price for his land,' declared Luther Drummond.

'Yes, But where's the money now?'

She looked directly at Dagg Drummond. 'Why pretend? You might just as well have shot him on his ranch. Comes to the same thing. You've stolen it from him.'

'My boy hasn't killed anyone,' declared Luther.

Her spirit buoyed by her husband's defiance, Ellen rejected this claim. 'Of course he has. I know it was him riding Mr Brodie's horse on the way to Gunner Pass. He killed Siggi and Claire's pa.'

'You can't prove that.'

Ethan spoke then. 'We can prove that he killed Johnny Harper.'

Luther's face clouded with fear. 'Johnny Harper. He's not dead.'

'We found his body a short time ago. Hidden on Diamond-D land.'

Dagg moved his hand towards his gun but again Claire moved her rifle in warning. 'What proof have you that I know anything about his death?' he asked.

'Claire,' Ethan said without losing

eye contact with Dagg, 'check that tall fellow's gunbelt. Tell me what you see.'

Curiously, Claire let her eyes scan Lou Petersen's midriff. When she saw the etched medallion hanging from the thong that was entwined around the belt, she gasped. All eyes turned to see what she had seen. Lou lifted the medallion and smiled, a thin, feral expression, like a cornered wolf preparing to attack. Dagg, all colour drawn from his face, staring at the reality of failure and a hangman's rope, growled at Lou. 'I told you to get rid of that.'

Aware that his son's words were confirmation of guilt, Luther's anguished expression revealed the extent of his fear. Too long accustomed to his word being law, he was shocked to realize that nothing he could say would prevent Dagg facing a charge of murder. Only action could save him now. 'You're not taking my boy,' he yelled to no one in particular. At the same time, with the intention of using her as a hostage while they made their escape, he reached down and grabbed Ellen Hartley's arm in an attempt to lift her on to his saddle.

Although reaching down made him a difficult target for Ethan and Claire, to John Hartley he presented a clear shot. The moment Luther grabbed his wife, John acted. Angrily, he snatched up the rifle that was propped near the open door. Sighting down the barrel he yelled Luther's name. That shout, a declaration of war as recognizable as any battlefield clarion, launched a brief explosion of violence.

Startled by the challenge, Luther glanced toward the hayloft and John discharged his rifle. The bullet hit Luther Drummond in the forehead, killing him instantly. Lou Petersen, proving faster on the draw than anyone suspected, fired in return, a reflex action, firing in the direction of the gun shot, his bullet hitting John who stumbled and toppled from the loft. As it registered with Claire that Lou had pulled out his gun, she squeezed the trigger of her Winchester and only a split second after shooting John Hartley, Lou took Claire's bullet in the abdomen. The force lifted him from his own horse, clear across the back of Luther's horse and dropped him on top of his dead boss.

Simultaneously, at the outbreak of gunfire, Dagg and Ethan went for their sidearms. Ethan was quickest. The distance between them was no more than six yards and a target the size of Dagg was too big for a skilled marksman to miss. Even so, Ethan put two bullets into his adversary. Dagg Drummond was dead before he hit the ground. The deaths of father and son were separated by little more than two seconds. Afterwards, all that was left was silence and the smell of gun smoke drifting and disappearing in the heat of the afternoon.

★　★　★

Sheriff Bob Cotton accompanied by his deputy Casey Drew and the new boss of the Diamond-D, Walt Benning, reached the Hartley ranch an hour later. Three bodies lay beneath the open hayloft door. Lou Petersen, despite the immediate administration of Doc Priestpole, died as a result of the gunshot inflicted by Claire Dumbril.

John Hartley survived. The bullet which struck him lodged against his right shoulder and, with Ellen's assistance, Doc Priestpole had it removed and the open wound dressed before the sheriff arrived. He'd also treated John's bumps and abrasions, the result of his fall from the loft. Fortunately, those injuries had been light because he'd landed on a pile of dirty straw raked earlier that day from the horse stalls below. Ellen fussed about, needing to treat her husband as her hero but unwilling to embarrass him while other people were around. He had fought for her, killed for her, and his only reward was a series of tender, discriminate touches as she tied the sling for his arm and brought him coffee. But for John those touches were enough, those and the looks that passed between them as she moved about the room.

Claire Dumbril's first reaction when she learned that Lou Petersen was dead was to lift her head a notch and stick out her chin, a demonstration that she wasn't ashamed of what she'd done, that she'd achieved the revenge she sought for the death of her father and Johnny Harper. But as the minutes passed a reaction set in and she sat alone in the far corner of the Hartleys' living room until Bob Cotton arrived. Ethan cast more than one glance in her direction but, until it was necessary for her to talk, chose to leave her to her own deliberation. Johnny Harper, he supposed, was foremost in her mind and any interruption by him would be unwelcome.

The events of the day, the attempted ambush, the discovery of Johnny Harper's body and the recent gunfight, were told to Bob Cotton by Ethan Brodie. Doc Priestpole, an independent witness, confirmed the details leading to the death of the Drummonds and Lou Petersen. Walt Benning's additional information confirmed Dagg Drummond's role in the stagecoach robbery so the sheriff confirmed that the law had been served by the killings here at the ranch. 'What now,' he asked Ethan as they walked out to the horses. 'Back to San Francisco?'

'Maybe.' Ethan looked across at Claire Dumbril who was talking quietly with Ellen Hartley. 'But I like the land here. Would be a good place to settle.' He excused himself and addressed Claire. 'Perhaps you'd be more comfortable riding back to town in the doctor's buggy.'

She gripped his sleeve and raised her head to look directly into his eyes. 'I rode in with you,' she said, 'any objections to having me ride back with you?'

We do hope that you have enjoyed reading this large print book.

Did you know that all of our titles are available for purchase?

We publish a wide range of high quality large print books including:
Romances, Mysteries, Classics
General Fiction
Non Fiction and Westerns

Special interest titles available in large print are:
The Little Oxford Dictionary
Music Book, Song Book
Hymn Book, Service Book

Also available from us courtesy of Oxford University Press:
Young Readers' Dictionary
(large print edition)
Young Readers' Thesaurus
(large print edition)

For further information or a free brochure, please contact us at:
Ulverscroft Large Print Books Ltd.,
The Green, Bradgate Road, Anstey,
Leicester, LE7 7FU, England.
Tel: (00 44) **0116 236 4325**
Fax: (00 44) **0116 234 0205**

CROOKED FOOT'S GOLD

Greg Mitchell

Jim and Barney are trailing a thief when they arrive at White Rock, but they become drawn into the mysterious community that is claimed by white gold-seekers and restless tribes alike. Then, a dying renegade tells them the story of Crooked Foot's gold, which leads to their being hunted down themselves, without knowing why. Now they must venture into dangerous territory seeking answers . . . and who knows what perils await them?

COUNT THE DEAD

Rick Dalmas

Dawson is thrown off a freight train, half-dead. But somehow, he eventually finds himself riding into a nearby town — astride a stranger's horse and with a dead man roped behind the cantle. Against all odds he gets a riding job with decent sidekicks. It looks good, but trouble awaits him, because, instead of tallying round-up steers, he is forced to fight for his very life.

NO QUARTER AT DEVIL'S FORK

Terrell L. Bowers

When Chilly Lloyd, a crazed outlaw, instigates a heinous crime, it seals the fate of seven other men. Now two friends, Brett Jackson and Reggie Satterfield, want to bring the killers to justice. Meanwhile, Stella Burdette agrees to run a chuck wagon for eight hunters — including Chilly Lloyd. But soon she must run for her life. And then Brett and Reggie fall into a deadly trap and are doomed to discover that there is *No Quarter At Devil's Fork*.